HARDCASTLE BOOKS

Skye's Fall

A TALE OF ELSEWHEN

THE JAIME SKYE CHRONICLES

BOOK 1

WILL FORREST

Book Cover and Layout by Hardcastle Books

Images licensed from Depositphotos

SKYE'S FALL: BOOK 1 OF THE JAIME SKYE CHRONICLES

ISBN: 978-1-990115-83-7

This edition includes the story THE MARVELOUS MR STRIKE: A TALE OF ELSE-WHEN

1st edition 2023

Many thanks to Day S Grant for their invaluable help in bringing this story to life

NOTE FOR READERS

Please be aware this book contains scenes of violence, and references to medical trauma, suicide, and the death of family members.

SKYE'S FALL

TAKEN

For the fifth time today, Cary Robb weighed the worth of murdering Lord High Magister Hercule Sandover. He'd be doing the world a favour to rid it of the odious mage, though it cost Cary his soul. If it was only his soul alone which hung in the balance.

The filth and noise of the Portsmouth dockyards—the thronging wharf-men and sailors, the horses and oxen and wagons and drays—disappeared behind the veil of memory: the cold stillness of the throne room, the Deathless Duke's voice creeping like a foul miasma, foretelling the spiritual exile awaiting him and all his kin should he fail in his singular duty.

He shook off the dire memory and followed Sandover, bound for the ship that would take them westward to the Americas where their ordeal would truly commence. They'd spent the day securing the last of the crew and cargo, Cary's role confined to standing at Sandover's elbow looking menacing as the Lord Magister did his business. All above board, but Sandover dressed like a Versailles fop, gauded up in last century's pink sateen knee-breeches and a tricorne with a plume amid the port town's flannel and canvas and muck, and was a ready target for thieves of all stripe.

Cary was there for the thieves' protection, for the mage was capable of killing with a thought and a snap of his manicured fingers, and he had left more than one eager-handed lout choking in the dirt. Dead men lead to complications, such as the police, who had to be paid off, or a thief's companions, who had to be threatened with worse violence. Better if they saw Cary at his side and thought twice about making the attempt.

Their ship was moored at the next wharf. As they rounded the corner of a warehouse, a shout of alarm rose from the water. Wharf-men and sailors leapt to secure the lines of their vessels, the masts of every ship in sight pitching back and forth as a freak wave struck the harbour. Seamen clung to the ropes of the tilting gangplank of their ship as another man—scrawny, panicked—scrambled on all fours towards solid ground.

Sandover cursed, baring his teeth. "Skye," he hissed. "You shan't escape me twice." He gripped Cary's sleeve. "Stop that man at once."

He nearly refused, for anyone clever enough to flee this doomed venture deserved their freedom. Skye was another matter, was the very reason for the venture, though the duke had not lowered himself to explain the man's purpose. Merely ordered Cary to keep Skye alive at any cost, and to not let him escape. One man's freedom against Cary's ancestors, his blood, all his dreamings.

He shook off Sandover's greedy hand and began to shove his way through the frantic dockyard towards the runaway. Pinned by a pair of drays heavily laden with sacks, Skye had hesitated. Cary reached for him, meaning to catch his arm, grabbing a handful of his short hair instead as he made to duck between the vehicles. As he shrieked and clutched at his head, Cary got an arm around his middle and yanked the slender bloke clear off his feet.

"Quit squirming, you ratbag," he grunted, letting go of Skye's sweat-dampened hair to thump him a good one on the side of the head. Groaning, the man sagged in Cary's grip as he lugged him up the gangplank. As Cary stepped onto the deck, Skye awoke in a frenzy, hissing and clawing at him like a feral cat, his sharp heels hacking at Cary's shins.

He grabbed Skye about the neck and slammed him against the cabin wall. The duke had spoken of this Jaime Skye as a fearsome mage of unparalleled power. If so, that power lay deep within, for he looked like a salamander found under a damp rock, gawping and pale, his reddish hair clinging to his scalp, sweat beading across his translucent forehead and cheeks despite the steady breeze.

"Get on with it then," he choked, his face pinched with bitter defiance. "Whatever it is you're going to do to me."

As if he expected the worst. As if this was not the first cruel hand he'd felt. With that familiar wrenching sense of justice ill-served, Cary yanked open the door to the bare, cramped cabin Sandover had prepared to contain both the man and his magic. He thrust Skye inside and shut the door, then latched it, barred it, and walked away.

Skye's waves began to ebb at once, though he had caused plenty of damage, spilling barrels and tumbling crates in the hold. Preparing to weigh anchor offered chores enough to keep Cary's hands occupied. Less so his mind, as Skye began begging. Not for mercy but for intervention. Louder and louder, until his screams reverberated through the very marrow of the ship: *don't let them take me.*

At last Skye's voice gave out. The clouds had lowered while the tugs had drawn their ship into the seaward current, and as the sails caught the wind, a miserable rain began to fall.

THE DOLDRUMS

For all he'd endured in the series of terrible events which passed for his life—the loneliness and dreariness, in and out of orphanages, foster homes, and asylums—Jaime Skye had never once known thirst. Hunger, yes, and of that far too much on this wretched voyage. The water his powers allowed him to draw from the air was enough to keep him alive but only barely. As he had more than once in his thirty-four years, he hoped this time he might die.

Slumped against the corner of the rank closet that served as his cabin, his chin resting on one up-bent knee, he shut his eyes against the assault of daylight as the door scraped open. His stomach tightened as the burnt treacle scent of Sandover's magic rolled over him.

"I don't care what state he's in." Though he spoke in English, Sandover's French birth was apparent in his sneering sibilance. "If this ship doesn't start to move, we'll not live to see landfall."

"You can bloody well fetch him yourself," the man known as Robb grunted through his teeth, his voice like tumbling rocks.

"With pleasure."

Jaime was flung into full awareness by a catastrophic pain, as though his very bones had caught alight and were burning him alive from the inside, eclipsing anything he'd suffered in his past. As quickly as it began, it ended, leaving him trembling and drenched with his peculiar sweat. A blessing and a curse of his condition, for more than once Sandover had 'bled' him in a similar fashion, torturing him then licking the salt-less water straight from Jaime's skin. A vile exploitation that transcended the merely physical.

"I can do that all day and night, Mr. Skye," the mage called from the door of Jaime's cell.

"I can't do what you want." Barely a breath, but the mage's ears had uncanny reach.

"You can and will. Bring him to the prow."

He might disobey Sandover's words, even his torture. He could do nothing to resist Robb's mighty grasp as he hoisted Jaime to his feet by his coat collar. His legs had cramped from so long in his huddled position, and hating his weakness he clung to the man's arm. A massive limb, hard as stone, tanned as leather. The arm was a piece with the man, his brow permanently furrowed, his woolly brown beard blurring the lower half of his even darker face as he half-dragged Jaime out of the miserable hatch where they kept him between Sandover's futile attempts to make him wake the water.

Futile because Jaime didn't know what to do. He'd had so few chances to learn how to use his powers, after a lifetime of being told they were a figment of his broken mind. For all he knew, everything that he'd achieved in that underground battle with Sandover had been Adrian's doing. Adrian's wishful thinking that Jaime was his equal in magical ability and not a conveniently placed madman.

Sandover didn't believe him. Or didn't care, and was hoping that Jaime would intuit the means by either luck or force of will, neglecting the fact that Jaime was more than happy to starve to death on this wretched ship in the middle of the Atlantic if only he could be sure of taking Sandover with him.

How long had they drifted in the doldrums? Two weeks? Three? He'd stopped counting days ago, for he so rarely saw the sky. No matter the day, Robb stayed Robb, and Sandover changed clothes every hour, and the rest of the crew stayed out of sight as best they could, for the mage's temper was vile and his punishments medieval.

Sandover was waiting at the prow dressed in pristine mauve silk, the fabric kept clean by magical means, for everyone else aboard stank like stable leavings. He smiled, not showing his teeth, for like several others his gums had begun bleeding now that the stores of fresh food had run out. Served the vainglorious shit right.

"Mr. Skye, I do wish you would be reasonable." Days of next to no water had dried Sandover's sweetly tuned voice to a witch's rasp.

"I told you, it's not a matter of reason," Jaime replied, his parched lips cracking anew. "I don't know what to do."

"That is a lie," Sandover hissed, a deadly light sparking in his eyes as his polite façade fell away. "I know you have power. I felt it when you emptied the canal."

"That was Lear's doing."

"There's no need to be humble, Mr. Skye," he said, smiling again. False to the core. "We could achieve so much working together. How can it serve you to refuse what I ask?"

"Anything that frustrates you serves my purposes."

"You do realize if we don't find some wind you'll be dead soon."

"So will you."

"You want to think that, but I've a deal with Sir Death. He works for me, you see? And now so do you."

"Go to hell."

This close, Sandover's magic hit with indescribable force, Jaime's shriek tearing at his arid throat as he fell writhing to the deck. At once it ended, the agony echoing through his limbs as Robb dragged him to his feet once more.

"Your choice, Skye. And don't even think about jumping overboard. I don't care how undrownable your damned family is, you'll starve to death before you reach land. If the sharks don't get you first, that is. Now where's that barrel?"

"He's no good to us dead," Robb grunted as Sandover wrenched Jaime from his grasp to frog-march him across the deck.

"He's not much good now," Sandover spat.

"Perhaps if you fed him—"

"He'll eat when he earns it."

The barrel of seawater stood waist-high and had sat open on the deck for a week. A salty green crust rimmed the inside of the barrel, the stench pummelling Jaime's overly sensitive nose. He braced his hands on the splintering rim as Sandover grabbed a handful of hair to force his head under the noxious water.

The first time he'd fought like the devil. Sandover had set him alight with pain then starved him for three days. He'd fight again, to the death. Sandover had taken everything he had, every friend, every comfort, every hope. The oily water seethed, ripples forming as he struggled against the wrenching grip on the back of his head.

"We don't have to do it this way, Mr. Skye," Sandover hissed. "I ask so very little."

"I can't do what you ask."

"Then suffer." Beyond summoning pain, Sandover's power allowed him control of others' bodies. Less so when one was endowed as Jaime was with Unordinary abilities, but he was sickened, weak, far from home and so wretchedly tired of fighting. A shade passed over

Sandover's grey eyes like the flick of a reptile's false eyelid as with a jolt Jaime's arms gave way. He shut his eyes and mouth as his head plunged beneath the surface. There was no way to close his nose, his sinuses inundated by the foul water.

The Skyes were undrownable. He knew it was so, had proved it to himself without a doubt, and yet he struggled, unwilling to give Sandover the least quarter, as his lungs burned and his face ached. Suddenly he was yanked upright. He fell to the deck to see Sandover and Robb standing off, Sandover's sunburnt face purple with rage.

"How dare you!" the mage shrieked in his hawk's rasp.

"You were killing him," Robb replied bluntly, his carven face inexpressive.

"No less than he's doing to me."

"Lay off him," Robb said more harshly as Sandover took a step towards Jaime. "I reckon he's telling the truth."

"And what do you reckon that on?" Sandover replied, though he came no closer.

"No man wants to die."

"Speak for yourself," Jaime croaked. Fool, such a fool, as with another savage shriek Sandover leapt upon him, grabbing him by the hair again.

"I knew it!" he snarled, shaking him so hard his teeth rattled. "You're doing this on purpose, aren't you? Killing us all along with yourself. How revoltingly selfish, Mr. Skye. Tell me, do you know what it means to keel-haul a man? Because I'd be very happy to demonstrate."

He dropped him again and stepped back. With a terrible smile he drew back his foot in its pointed slipper, preparing to kick Jaime in the stomach. He froze with his foot suspended in the air, his face in a rictus of conflicting emotions, the smile belied by the panic in his wheeling eyes. Unbalanced, he tumbled to one side, hitting the deck with a pinched wheeze of agony.

Then Robb's massive hands were under Jaime's arms as he lifted him. Higher, laying Jaime's limp body across his plank of a shoulder as he started for the hatch that would take them below.

THE MINDER

In the cramped forward hold, Cary propped a moaning Skye on a crate to strip off his fouled shirt. He wiped his face and neck clean of the scum from the barrel while Skye batted at him with limp hands.

"Why did you do that?" he asked in a breathy sigh, the words sliding into one another. "Why did you stop him."

Not *how*, but *why*. "Because I need you alive."

"If you have such power...why haven't you killed him?"

"I need him alive, too. He has something I want."

"Stolen, no doubt," Skye breathed with a hint of a laugh. Cary said nothing. It wasn't Skye's business. "Like I was," he went on. "I shouldn't have left him. Adrian, I'm so sorry..."

Then he was gone into sleep, his features slackening before Cary's eyes. So starved he was that Cary lifted him as easily as a child. He laid Skye in his own hammock, where the poor bugger curled up and started shivering though the hold was as stifling as ever.

He had just settled a woollen blanket over Skye when Sandover's poncy slippers came clacking down the ladder. The rotter paused in the square of sunlight falling through the hatch, which bleached Sandover's face back to its northern pallor, his fair hair glowing like a froth of wattle blossoms. He was a cesspit.

"That was a clever little trick, Mr. Robb," he said in his cawing rasp.

"I'd stay there if I were you. It's dangerous down here in the dark."

"It's not you I'm here to see."

"Which is why you ought to keep to yourself."

"Have you've forgotten who's in command?"

"I haven't forgotten, I just don't bloody care. And you'd do well to remember whose command *you're* under. What will the duke say if you damage his toy?"

Sandover's rage shimmered hotly, but Cary had the read of him. The man was foul but insignificant, a fly buzzing around an open wound, as much a slave as Cary to their dreadful master, who could crush them all with a thought, raise the ship from the water and dash it to bits on the nearest island, or simply submerge them. A man who could have magicked his way across the sea, and instead sent his servants to risk their lives in his place.

"If I'm to mind Skye, he stays where I can see him," Cary said, daring Sandover to overstep and give him an excuse. Any excuse, even if it saw them all sent to Davy Jones.

"If he should escape—"

"To bloody where?"

Sandover didn't blink. "If he should, it shall be you who suffers his grace's displeasure, Mr. Robb."

He performed a courtly bow, all twirling wrists and simpering, then scurried up the ladder. Skye hadn't stirred, his shoulders rising and falling naturally under the fraying blanket. Sleep would do him right. Hopefully he'd find his way into a good dream.

Cary hadn't had much luck finding any for himself. Then again he'd been away from his country for close on four years. He could sense the landscape beneath them, great mountains and valleys to dwarf those above the surface of the water, their fragile ship a twig in a flood.

Sandover was right, even if Skye survived immersion, the poor bugger would never reach land. Things got strange in the deep. Cary had seen enough impossible creatures dragged up from the bottom of the sea to know it was a place unlike the world of humankind. Some mysteries weren't meant to be solved.

S kye woke as the sun was setting, its ruddy light leaving the hold in velvet gloom. Cary lit a lantern and hung it from a peg behind Skye's head so it wouldn't pain the man's eyes. After helping him upright, Cary found him a scrap of hard bread.

"Don't bother biting it or you'll lose your teeth," he cautioned as Skye clutched the crust in both hands. "Suck on a bit till you can swallow it. Make it last."

"And you?"

"I'm right."

"But are you hungry? I could share this."

"You need your strength."

"Thank you. And for earlier."

As Skye began nibbling on a corner of the crust Cary got out his pipe. He mixed a few grains of numbing greysand with some ordinary sailor's tobacco and stepped to the porthole to smoke it. He had girth enough to go without a meal, while Skye was so slim he might blow away on the next stiff breeze. As he returned, Skye began coughing.

"You right?"

"You put something in your tobacco," he wheezed.

"I didn't think you'd notice."

"It's one of my...things. Problems."

"Your sense of smell is a problem?"

"Some say gift. I can smell Sandover's magic. Yours smells different." He had finished the bit of bread and lay back in the hammock, his slight form disappearing beneath the edge.

"Is it so, what you're telling him?" Cary asked the invisible man. "That you don't know how to use your skills?"

"Skills?" came the murmured answer.

"Talent, power, nature…it's all the same thing. I've seen him work you over for your sweat."

"That's as may be, but I'm sure I don't know how to move the ocean."

"Maybe you don't have to move all of it." Cary been thinking about it for the past few days. Country measured days and years between the flows and ebbs of water crossing the landscape. What was the ship but a hunk of the land crossing water? "Just move the bit behind us. Ask it to give us a shove. That'll get us going. That's the thing with water, it wants to move, wants to flow. It's no happier here in the doldrums than we are." He said nothing more, going about his quiet business while Skye lay in the hammock, hopefully thinking.

"You were right," the hammock said at length. "I don't want to die. Not here, not like this." He grabbed the edge to pull himself upright. "Help me above-decks and I'll…I'll see what I can do."

SUBMISSION

erhaps it was the piquant scent of Robb's tobacco or simply the sunlight, but Jaime's sickly despair began to lift as he came up onto the deck. If they weren't starving to death in the doldrums it would have been a glorious day, the water sparkling prettily, the sun gleaming off the pale canvas. Sandover was loitering amidships, wearing a coat of bright blue silk embroidered with white lilies. The same coat he'd worn the day they had met, in the halls of the Magisters' Club. Jaime had seen through his polish and politeness in a twinkling.

"Ah, Mr. Skye, how good of you to join us," he sneered with a supercilious bow. "Wait, the prow is this way."

"I'm going to try it from the stern," Jaime said as he started up the short ladder to the quarterdeck. "Not so sure why, I just had a sense."

"And why should I trust your senses?"

"I've watched you try to raise the wind," Robb said, following him up the ladder. "You don't know what to do either."

The short climb cost Jaime much of his strength. Holding tight to the rail, he made his way to the stern. There lay home, some thousands of miles to the east, below the shimmering horizon. He put it from his mind and turned his attention to the vague hummocks of the unstirred sea immediately behind the ship. The water was trapped like they were, the flow incoherent, pushed by the contra-factual winds of the world and the currents of the greater ocean into this stagnant pocket of immobility.

Rise, he thought. *A little swell. A little push, nothing fancy. Rise and set us all free.* Trapped with Adrian in the flooded tunnel of the Huddersfield canal, he'd pictured it in his mind's eye, pictured the water swirling, whirling, simmering into vapour and escaping through the ventilation shafts. Now he thought of waves, the way they piled one upon another as they crossed the sea, became one great swell that caused the tides and ruled the lives of sailors and whales and all the earth, more sea than land, a water world.

Rise and set us free. He closed his eyes, throwing all his awareness into believing that his mere thoughts had power. That nature felt his heartfelt need and could not help but answer. There, surely, the feel of the deck shifting under his feet, the creak of the spars as the stern of the ship lifted.

"*Incroyable...*" Sandover whispered from close behind him. Jaime said nothing, his hands gripping the rail, his whole mind devoted to his plea. Sandover's vile scent was all over him, the raw stink of unwashed flesh and the burnt sugar stench of his magic.

Then Sandover touched him. Not merely touched him but grabbed his skull between his hands. An infusion of scorching power tore through him, Jaime's stomach lurching as the deck tilted sharply. He forced his eyes open as the stern suddenly dipped.

A wake of ten foot swells was racing towards the ship. Sandover cackled, his touch its own horror, as if his fingers were embedded in Jaime's brain. As the first great wave struck the ship Sandover was hurled against him. The mage laughed again, his grip unyielding, a telling pressure against Jaime's backside.

The devil was hard. He was loving this. His nails stabbing into Jaime's scalp, he began to thrust, shoving himself against Jaime in an awful rhythm driven by the terrifying pitch and yaw of the ship. At last the sounds of the other seamen reached Jaime's ears, their panicked shouts and the tumble of barrels and trunks, the boom and flap of dry sails being filled as the ship was driven by the unnatural waves as if before a hurricane.

He could do nothing to stop it, Sandover's possession of him absolute, his body encased in a searing immobility. He was going to die, catch alight from the inside, the golden light of Adrian's healing touch a candle to this conflagration. And then it stopped, and Sandover stepped away, panting.

Jaime fell to the deck and started to retch. He felt naked and pummelled, as if Sandover had not just rubbed against him but been inside his helpless body. Sandover's satin slippers appeared in front of him, and if only Jaime had something in his guts to vomit over them.

"There, that wasn't so hard, was it, Mr. Skye?" Sandover drawled from above. "Get some food into him and put him away. I'll have need of him again."

Once more Robb bundled him up and carried him below, where he lay in the big hammock and shivered, drifting in and out of consciousness. Whenever Jaime woke, Robb was beside him, engaged in his business with herbs and dirt or simply sitting cross-legged on a crate, seeming half asleep but rising when Jaime stirred.

"You ready for some tucker?"

His word for food. He helped Jaime upright then gave him another sliver of hard bread. "I didn't know how to stop him," he said as Jaime sucked on the corner. "I thought it might hurt you more if I yanked him away."

"Never mind. It worked, didn't it?"

"Because of you. His highness just about tipped the bloody boat over."

Jaime's mouthful of bread was a sodden mush, but as soon as he swallowed it, his stomach rebelled. Robb had a bucket ready, and a cloth to wipe his mouth. Jaime fell back groaning, his head thumping with pain. The agony was relentless, a bodily ache that went down to his bones, like the worst stages of morphine withdrawal. He retched again as a cloud of Sandover's stink rolled over him.

"*Alors*? Is he mended?" the magister asked as he descended the ladder into the hold.

"Leave him alone," Robb growled from the shadows.

"I only want to thank him," Sandover said. In the gloom he was a death's head, his eyes black pits, his smile fixed as he wound his way around the crates. "We've a marvellous wind behind us now. He should be very proud."

"You can stop right there," Robb said. "He can hear you well enough. Say what you've got to say then bugger off."

"May I not shake his hand?" Sandover oozed, his smell creeping across Jaime's skin like oily dew.

"Don't let him touch me."

"There," Robb said, crossing his arms over his massive chest. "You heard the man."

Sandover halted, his smell thickening in the air. "You think you're very clever, don't you, Mr. Robb?"

"I know my place. Keeping him in one piece until the job is done. It's bloody hard work when you feel the need to suck him dry."

"I have only the best intentions, Mr. Robb."

"Your intentions can get stuffed."

"You don't understand," Sandover said, desperation icing his voice. "I need to touch him. I need to feel it again."

"No."

"Damnation, you don't know what it's like."

"Don't care, either. You did it to yourself. You can manage by yourself."

With a barely throttled shriek Sandover lunged, but Robb was ready with a handful of dust which he flung at the mage. Sandover recoiled, swatting at the air as the dust swirled around him, motes glittering in the beam of sunset light that chose that moment to break through the distant clouds. Pursued as if by a swarm of enraged wasps he scurried for the ladder, spitting out dust and cursing Robb and Jaime both.

THE GIFT

They rode before a fair wind for two days. While Skye slept, Cary shifted the crates into a barricade to make it visible to Sandover how unwelcome he was. There were two holds on the ship, this the fore and smaller. None of the crew had objected when he claimed it for himself. He was used to making people uneasy. Depended on it at times, his brute strength a shield, his stoic stare a blunt weapon, able to crush any argument. He'd never thought to meet a harder man than himself until he'd met the duke.

The mere thought of that demon in human form made Cary's hackles rise, for it was the duke who'd made Cary servant to that ratbag Sandover. The duke who held Cary's spirit hostage and had made him poor Skye's jailor. And now protector.

Skye meanwhile thrived on his scanty diet of hard bread, fish, and the water he plucked from the air the way Cary drew dust and smoke. A bag of bones, a scarecrow, this Jaime Skye, his ruddy hair a ragged, salt-burnt thatch, his bright eyes hiding terrifying depths, glowing like candle flames in the gloom of the creaking hold.

Evening was falling on the third day, the sunset stretching its rosy arms across the water and piercing the port-side portholes. The motion of the ship was beginning to wear on Cary, and he'd been leaning on his stocks of sand, keeping his stomach numbed with greysand and his head clear with red. Bad habits, but why else had he hoarded these treasures for so many miles if not to use them in his time of need?

"You mind?" Cary said, taking out his pipe.

Skye shook his head. "Not at all. I'd rather smell that than sweat and tar and you-know-who."

Before tamping the tobacco, Cary tipped in a few grains of grey. "I keep meaning to ask," Skye said as Cary peered inside the pouch. "If those are flavorings or part of your magic."

"The latter. Though it does give it a taste."

"Is that how you tell them apart?"

He chuckled, thinking of the folk he'd seen undone by black wattle. "It's usually too late if you have to taste 'em to know."

"Is it dangerous?"

"Anything can be dangerous if you do it wrong."

"True. I don't even drink."

"Does it affect your talent?"

"I wouldn't know. I didn't know I had talent, as you say, until a few weeks ago."

Cary paused, the lit match hovering over the tobacco. "Didn't know? How could you not?"

"I thought I was out of mind. That it was my imagination running away with itself." He exhaled slowly, his jaw trembling. "It wasn't easy lying to myself but I did it. For thirty years."

"'Struth."

"It's a wonder I don't drink. Perhaps I ought to start. Or try your tobacco. Do you suppose I would enjoy it?"

"It's not a matter of enjoy. This is medicine."

"Are you sick?"

"I would be. This far from land." Even further from his home, his country, the land that had birthed him. The place he belonged like nowhere else. The place he had left behind, out of shame, out of need, out of selfish pride.

"We'll be across soon," Skye said. "Four days, no more."

"How do you know that?"

"I...don't know," he said with a wrinkle in his brow. "There's so much I don't know."

As he lay back in the hammock, the hatch in the deck swung open on its wooden hinge. A pair of bare feet descended the ladder. They were attached to the putative cabin boy Leody, a stammering lad of no more than sixteen who obeyed Sandover like a whipped dog. He'd been press-ganged into service in a Portsmouth alleyway by Cary himself, when the Philippines-born lad had offered to perform an illegal act for the shamefully low price of a hot dinner from the nearest stall. Like many aboard, his clothes were bleached to ragged paleness, his pretty little face darker than Cary's own. He stood at the bottom of the ladder blinking in the pink light.

"What's he want now?" Cary asked.

The lad jumped, grabbing for the ladder, then with a fearful glance upward let go. "To be sure of Mr. Skye," he answered, looking about the unlit hold for Cary, who hadn't moved from his shadowy perch on a barrel on the starboard side. "That he's being cared for properly."

"Better than he ever did," Skye said bitterly from inside the gently swaying hammock. "I did what he asked, moved the ship."

"And he wants to thank you."

Skye's tousled head appeared. "If he's so grateful, he can turn this ship around and take me home."

"Why did Sandover send you and not come himself?" Cary asked Leody, who looked like he might cry, biting his lips and twisting the hem of his threadbare shirt in both hands.

"He says he'll give you a better cabin," he blurted, ignoring Cary. "A bigger share of the rations. Anything you want. Anything."

"Comfort?" Cary said.

"Yes."

"Obedience? Yours, for example?"

"Is that why he sent you?" Skye said with alarm, sitting upright in the hammock. "As a bribe? To tempt me into trusting him?"

The poor boy had turned to stone, except for the panicked rise and fall of his belly, visible through a great rent in his shirt. Bloody Sandover, trying to barter with this poor lad's body. Yet another cause to despise him.

"You're barking up the wrong tree," Cary said. "No one down here needs that kind of comfort."

"He's delusional," Skye said as he fell back in the hammock.

"He is, you know," Leody said in an urgent hiss, stepping away from the ladder into the dark. "He talks to his mirror. Won't touch iron. Keeps all his tea leaves."

"What does he have on you?" Cary asked.

With another frightened glance above, the boy shook his head then stepped back into the square of light.

"Please, don't go," Skye said, struggling upright again. "I expect he said he'd do something dreadful to you if you didn't deliver."

"He'll do something dreadful anyway." He scrambled up the ladder and was gone.

Neither man spoke for some time, as if waiting for the sound of Sandover's retribution. The thud of a body striking the deck, or a scream, though with the mage's skill he could stop your tongue, make you burn in silence. At length Skye sighed and began to struggle his way out of his canvas cocoon. Cary went to help him, but when he made to scoop him up like a child Skye waved him off.

Clinging to Cary's arm, he heaved himself out of the hammock with surprising strength for the feather weight of him. "I shouldn't hide away," he said, gripping a spar overhead as he swayed with the ship. "I can't let Sandover think he rules me."

"Might not be the worst thing, though."

"How can you say that?"

Skye was shorter than him by a foot or more and Cary had to bend to speak close to his ear. "I reckon what's best is for us to get across as quick as can be. Once we're on dry land, we'll sort ourselves out."

"Ourselves," Skye replied in the same half-formed whisper. "Hmm."

"You and me together, we're the strongest thing going." Sandover's touched ears could hear a fart in a thunderstorm, and rather than explain Cary cupped his hand and set a dust devil whirling.

Skye's eyes grew enormous as he watched the hot swirl rise and fall, the tiny storm tracking a ragged circle on Cary's palm. "Well," he murmured. "How very interesting."

THE STORM

Where Sandover smelled of burnt cake, this man smelled like fire. Like the scent of his tobacco had invaded every pore of his skin, a spiced, sappy aroma with a musky undertone wholly foreign to Jaime's oversensitive nose. In the brown fugue of the hold, Robb seemed almost a part of the ship, a carven beam that had learned to walk and talk, his blunt features speaking of the ancient tree he would have been.

"Does he know you can do that?" Jaime asked as Robb let the miniature whirlwind subside, the swirling motes disappearing as they settled on his palm.

"He knows a little."

"But not all."

"No."

Then Sandover's control was not absolute. Immense depths lurked beneath this man Robb's imperturbable surface, his face stiff as carved wood, his eyes lost in shadow. Yet Jaime felt no fear, the musky scent of Robb's magic evoking a sense—half a wish, half a memory—of soaring skies above a sun-soaked plain. So far he had saved Jaime twice from Sandover's cruelty, and once from his malignant breed of kindness in the form of that poor lad Leody. Yet by every other measure he was Sandover's servant.

"Will you help me get above?" Jaime asked.

Robb frowned. "Why?"

"I'll wear myself out getting past these boxes."

"No, why do you want to go up there?"

"I know it puts me nearer to him but I'm going stir-crazy. Might be nice to get some air."

Standing at his full height, Robb's bushy hair touched the beams. He gazed at Jaime, his nostrils flared, his eyes shadowed beneath his hard brow. "As you like," he grumbled. "But stick close."

To see the sky was like greeting a friend. Happily, Sandover wasn't about, so Jaime stood at the rail and let the air wash over him, drying the sour sweat from his back, ruffling his hair which had grown out from his customary crop into an unbecoming cap of reddish-brown straw. But he was alive, and no longer so acutely alone.

Robb was speaking with the ship's cook. Jaime started tacking along the rail towards them, his stomach griping with the first genuine pangs of hunger since Sandover's abuse of him and his subsequent collapse.

As the deck tilted sharply he halted, unsure of his legs. The wind was changing course, the spars creaking as the sails billowed against them. A pair of swabs started up the sheets to trim the canvas. The sky's blue was thickening, moisture massing on the forward horizon. Robb came to meet him.

"You feel it too?"

A soft thrumming impulse passed over them, a sound that wasn't wholly there. "What on earth was that?" Jaime asked.

"Maybe a storm's coming."

"I need to see more of the sky." He followed the flick of Robb's eyes upward to the top, a miserly platform built halfway up the main mast. "How do I get up there?"

Robb frowned. "You'll blow away."

"Then tie a rope around my waist. If there's a storm coming we ought to know."

Robb relented, though as Jaime climbed higher up the shrouds he began to wish he hadn't insisted, for the wind was ferocious, snatching and shoving at him. On reaching the top he merely clung to the mast at first, but as the ship began climbing a wave he got to his feet, his fingers knotted in the ropes.

As the ship slid down the back of the wave he saw the storm. Not saw, more like felt, for it had yet to breech the horizon. But everything spoke of it: the massing sky, the sucking wind, the dampness of the air as the clouds drew water. Another ineffable tremor shuddered across the heaving sea. Yet on they sailed, their pace undiminished even with the sails trimmed.

Behind the ship, a long wave stood like a foam-topped rampart, never breaking as it raced towards them. Sandover's work, he was sure of it, driving them onward unnaturally. Directly into the storm.

Jaime slithered down in more haste than he'd climbed. "We're sailing into disaster," he told Robb, who was waiting on the deck with Captain Warner. "Is Sandover propelling the ship?"

"He must have kept your spell alive," Robb rumbled.

"He needs to stop. Or we need to turn aside."

"I'm inclined to agree with you, Mr. Skye," Warner said. "There's some mickle oddness in the air a'day." A glum-faced man of middling age with wiry grey sideburns and a persistent stoop, Captain Warner seemed better suited to piloting a canal barge than navigating oceans.

He had however an impressive bellow and had all hands on deck in seconds.

As the crew leapt to ready the ship for the weather, Sandover emerged from his cabin below the fo'c'sle. Dressed in a sickly shade of yellow, he yawned hugely, then noticed the hubbub. "What are you doing?" he cried, grabbing at the nearest sailor. "I told you full sail!"

"Captain says—"

"Blast the captain!" Sandover hissed. "You'll do as I say! Full sail ahead."

"We'll be dashed to pieces," Warner barked from above him. "That's no ordinary storm."

"Yes, but he's no ordinary man," Sandover replied as he started up the ladder. "Are you, Mr. Skye?"

"You want me to stop that?" The storm had cleared the horizon and now bore down upon them, a vast wall of bruised purple clouds, the rain a seething grey curtain hanging below. The choppy waves were growing, crashing against the hull, the spray hanging in the air like sour mist. A world of water, and Jaime was one little man, with the barest inkling of how to use his power.

"Not stop," Sandover said with a mirthless smile as he approached them. "Deter. Push a little off its course so that we needn't abandon ours. Surely your immense capabilities can render us this small service."

"I can't possibly—"

The smile died. "You will, Mr. Skye, or I'll strap you to the mast and let the storm have you."

"It's having us either way if we don't change our heading," Warner said. As he started for the ladder Sandover made a careless gesture over his shoulder. Warner slumped, clutching his chest, trembling as his face turned a violent shade of red.

"Your opinions are not of interest, Captain," Sandover said, his dreadful eyes on Jaime. "I said full sail." He snapped his fingers and Warner staggered forward, leaning his hands on his knees as he gasped for breath. "Well?"

"Aye, Mr. Sandover," Warner wheezed.

"As for our Mr. Skye," Sandover said with another false smile that made Jaime take a good step back. "I tried to be nice. I offered you the very best of everything. And you refuse me. Why, when this could be so much easier if you did as I asked?"

"I can't do it."

"Yes, but I can."

"You leave him alone," Robb said, stepping in front of Jaime as the mage reached for him, a vile hunger in his glassy eyes.

"Interfere again, Mr. Robb, and I shall burn out your tongue."

"Let me speak to him."

"If you dare counsel mutiny—"

"This ain't the Bounty and you're not bloody Captain Bligh. Just let me have a word." Before Sandover argued further, Robb steered Jaime to the prow. Here the dip and rise of the waves was violently apparent, the spray stinging his face and soaking his thin shirt.

"You know he'll torture you," Robb said in a low rumble that matched the oncoming thunder.

"I know."

"The sooner we get across, the sooner you can be free of him."

"I'll never be free of him."

"We will. I promise."

"If we live."

"That'll have to be your department. I haven't much muster this far from land."

"I can't speak to the wind."

"Not even if that wind's full of water? And what's the worst that could happen?" he went on as Jaime merely stared at the hell-storm. "You give it a go and get nowhere."

"The worst is that all of us die."

"So you've got nothing to lose, am I right?"

What else could he do? He wanted so much to believe Robb. To believe in himself as well. Sandover's confidence meant nothing, for the man was clear out of his mind. Jaime had met many people in similar states of derangement over his many sanatorium stays. Men poisoned by megalomania, driven by unspeakable demons, terrorizing all who fell into their sphere. There seemed little to be done for most aside from sedate them and keep them from hurting others.

Yet he had thought the same of himself for most of his life, believing that his strange fits, his elevated senses were proof not of an innate ability to command the forces of nature but a special kind of mania. That these powers he had only just begun to understand were a delusion or at best a lie. None of those unfortunates in the wards had had Sandover's powers.

Himself, however...

The worst was that nothing happened at all. The worst was that Sandover killed them today, not through malice but through a lack of seamanship. Jaime had craved oblivion often enough that he'd blunted his fear of it. All who were born would someday die, and most had no say in the how or the when. Jaime would die on his feet, fighting to save his life. Not just him but the sailors, the captain, the cook. Cary Robb, who had saved him. Sandover, so that Jaime might bring him to justice. Yet the storm was so huge it might have been a god. An ancient god of the netherworld, all-consuming, all-destroying, indifferent to even the most fervent prayers.

Spare us

Spare us, we poor, unguarded, helpless human lives
Spare us and we'll leave you be, leave the ocean to you
Oh sky, oh rain, oh endless, endless sea
Please spare us...

Clinging to the rail, he thought it again and again, as Sandover's will drove them onward, the waves nearly cresting over the prow in the mad pitch of the ship. The mountainous storm wall was rotating, the wind catastrophic, and all Jaime had was his will, a tiny flame against an apocalypse. As the deck tipped alarmingly he fell to his knees, his hands slipping on the soaked wood rail. Much longer and he'd be washed away by the next heavy wave. He could not despair, for the sake of their lives, but the storm was beyond him.

Spare us...

Something fell on his shoulder. Something heavy and warm and solid, the warmth flowing into Jaime like pure water into a dry river. He opened his eyes and saw the storm anew. The currents, the torsion, the shape of the winds, as if sketched in skeleton, diagrammed: a patent for a new style of hurricane. Unwilling to look away he touched his cheek to the hand on his shoulder, smelled the arid warmth of Robb's skin, his the heat warming Jaime's heart.

Spare us...

Digging his fingernails into the wood Jaime shoved himself to his feet. Robb kept hold of him, his other hand braced on the rail, his body shielding Jaime from Sandover. "Don't give up," Robb hollered over the bludgeoning wind. "Or we're all for the deep."

Spare us...

MUTINY

Cary knew storms like this were real. He'd journeyed through the northern straits after a cyclone's passage and been sickened by the damage, whole shorelines toppled from the wind, what remained of the Kala and Miriam settlements strewn like ashes. Towering above them, this storm could have swallowed a mountain as its twisting wind drew their pathetic ship deeper into its deadly grip, the ocean's surface seeming to boil as the clouds sucked up even more water.

Connected to Skye's elemental power, he could not only feel the weight of water in the air but see it, the thousand thousand tiny motes of vapour constituting every cloud. A galaxy, and they one tiny scrap of starlight.

Skye was shaking under Cary's hand. "This is impossible," he cried as the force of his will faltered. "This storm's like nothing on earth."

"Sandover's foxing your spell, driving us into the wind," Cary shouted over the roar of wind and wave.

"I can't help that!"

"Have you tried?"

"Have you?"

"I'm busy keeping you alive. But if the two of us can't turn a storm, perhaps it can't be turned."

"Then we're doomed!"

"Forget the bloody storm, what of the sea?" Cary shouted as Skye's shoulders fell. "How did you save us before?"

"Asked for its help."

"What if you did that again? There's plenty of water that isn't this."

"If only we could steer."

"Then let's go where we can."

He tucked a sputtering Skye under his arm and started for the stern, struggling against the pitch of the deck, the belt of cold waves and the needling spray, the growing sense that this was beyond hopeless. Two figures swayed above them on the quarterdeck, though it wasn't clear through the haze if they were fighting each other or merely the ship. As one fell, the other made a slithering dash for the ladder.

Sandover, who reached the mizzen mast as they did. In the storm or the struggle he'd bloodied his nose, dark stains streaking his soaking wet suit, his pale hair whipping about in snaky strands.

"What are you doing?" he shrieked. "Get back to your post."

Before they could answer, another vast wave struck. Frigid water washed over the canting deck, surging around Cary's ankles and knocking Sandover's feet from under him and throwing him hard against the far rail. A great yawning moan shook the ship as the crooked mage's spell fell apart.

They now rode rudderless, the deck tilting violently sideways as Cary and Skye crawled towards the quarterdeck. There they found Captain Warner lying in a crumpled heap. They hadn't time to see if he still lived as the ship struck the face of the next mountainous wave.

On hands and knees they reached the helm. As Skye grasped the great wheel he cried out, not in terror but a sort of joy. "I feel it! You were right." He hauled himself to his feet, gripping the pegs fiercely. Cary followed more cautiously, for the ship pitched wildly beneath them, at the mercy of the elements, the wind and waves and the suck of the deep.

"Keep hold of me," Skye shouted as he cut the wheel hard a' starboard. "I can't do this alone." Easy to believe when the scrawny bloke could barely see over the wheel. As before, Cary laid his hand on Skye's shoulder, the connection rooting deep into his astral body. Skye shouted again, fiercely joyful. Now they moved with the ship and the ship moved with the sea, riding the dip and surge of the living water. Skye was laughing, and Cary would have given anything to see it.

Slipping through the troughs, skirting the wind, they sailed northwest at impossible speeds, the storm slipping further and further a' port, until the water in the air was pure rain and not spray and the sky was black not with clouds but with night.

"Is it done?" Skye mumbled.

"It's done."

"That's good." His hands slipped from the pegs, his legs folding neatly beneath his unconscious weight. Cary had just enough presence of mind to grab him before his head hit the deck.

Warner had woken some hours ago and was well enough to take the helm. His legs quivering with exhaustion, Cary lifted poor Skye onto his shoulder as before and carried him belowdecks. He'd yet to fix a second hammock, and simply clambered into his own with Skye's narrow body wedged beside him. Slept.

Woke with a feral cat in his lap, hissing as it fought to get out from under his arm. No, it was Skye swatting at him in the midst of a panicked dream. As he caught Skye's flailing hand the man woke.

"Why are you here?" he asked, blinking in the half-light.

"This was all there was."

Skye sat up then lay back at once and covered his face. "Ugh. That's an unpleasant sensation."

"I reckon you're hungry after all that."

"Please, no more crusts."

"No worries. There aren't any more."

"Well. That's helpful." He sat up more slowly, then with Cary's help clambered out of the hammock. Cary followed, though he could have slept for another decade. The hold echoed with the thump of bare feet, the creak and clunk of masts and spars, sunlight freckling through the gaps in the planks. They had weathered the storm or outrun it.

"That was well done, Skye, to get us through."

"Please, call me Jaime. You've done so much for me, I'd like to consider you a friend."

"Even though my job is making sure you don't run away?"

"Where am I going to go? But I've gathered that you're not part of this expedition by choice."

Cary grunted, neither a yes or a no, unwilling to burden Jaime with the facts of his indentured state, but Jaime was satisfied, holding out his hand. "So, Mr. Robb, are we friends?" he asked.

"Call me Cary."

They shook, Jaime's quick grasp softly damp, like he'd been walking in the mist. He was about to speak when the shouting started. Evidently Sandover, to judge from the pitch, though his words were impossible to make out, muffled by the thick wooden deck.

"Suppose we ought to see what that's about," Cary said, very much wanting to do the opposite.

"Did he run out of wig powder?" Jaime said, tucking in his shirt.

"Tore his stockings?"

"Soiled his breeches?"

They broke up in childish, snorting laughter. Sandover's garbled tirade continued as they mounted the ladder. Perhaps he'd knocked his head and gone even further out of it. The cause was even more satisfying, for Sandover had been gagged and tied to the main mast.

"I was wrong. You are Captain Bligh," Cary said as Sandover glared at them over the rag wound around the lower half of his face.

"O-uu-ehhh" the mage howled, his meaning clear from the livid red of his forehead, the bulge of his eyes.

"What's that?" Cary said, cupping his ear. "I couldn't make out what you said."

"Don't tease him," Jaime said as Sandover thrashed against his bonds. The crew had taken no chances, tying his arms over his head but far apart, then winding both hands and his torso with what looked like every spare rope on board, glimpses of his filthy yellow coat visible between the coils. He looked exactly as miserable as he deserved, and it was strongly tempting to ignore him and let sun and starvation do their worst, but if Cary wanted his liberty, he needed Sandover alive. The mage had continued to shriek through his gag as they approached, and Cary stretched out a tendril of subtle force to wrap around his tongue and silence him.

"We can resolve this in one of two ways," he said as Sandover's eyes swelled with indignation. "Either you mind your manners, let the captain steer the ship, and keep your filthy hands off Mr. Skye, or you can spend the rest of the voyage in this exact state, minded by me. By the time we make landfall you'll be broiled like a side of beef and twice as mad as you already are. Your choice, but make it quick." He tugged down the cloth, undid the second gag between Sandover's teeth, then unleashed his tongue.

"You dare to threaten me?" the mage shrieked. He screamed again as Cary pinched not his tongue but his testicles in his subtle grip.

"All right, Captain Bligh. Have it your way. Enjoy explaining to his grace how you duffed up his little venture by playing the fool." He released his invisible hold and Sandover slumped in his bonds.

"Come back!" he cawed as Cary began walking away. "Damn you, I said come back! Oh *merde*...parlay! Parlay!"

THE ST LAWRENCE

By Jaime's influence or perhaps only luck, they found a fair wind and made up for some of their lost days. They saw very little of Sandover for the rest of the trip. Morale among the crew improved in direct proportion.

Jaime and Cary were out on deck after supper one evening when the cabin boy emerged from Sandover's cabin with a tray. The mage barely seemed to eat and tonight was no different, a thin film glazing the surface of the murky stew.

"He didn't touch it, did he?" Cary asked, pausing as he went to take the bowl from Leody.

"He wouldn't even let me put it down. It's all yours, Mr. Robb."

"We'll share it," Jaime said as Cary passed it to him.

"I'm not hungry," he grunted.

"You're twice my size."

"Only because you're skin and bones."

"Something no amount of feeding has ever changed."

"That'll be the work," he said as Jaime took the spoon from him. "Burns you up. Me, I got fuel to spare. Anything else to report?" he asked Leody who stood fidgeting with the empty tray.

"That he's still writing that letter."

"Or a new one," Jaime said. It seemed the mage did nothing else, his enchanted pen producing endless ink with no sign of an inkwell.

"If so, where are they?" Cary said. "I've searched that room. There's not a board loose. So where's he sticking them?"

"Out the porthole?" Jaime offered, hunting through the gravy for the last bits of onion.

"Maybe he eats them," Leody said with a wild grin.

"That'd explain why he walks around like he's got a cork up his arse," Cary replied. Leody giggled, his tongue pushing at the gap in his front teeth.

"What do you reckon he's up to?" Cary asked Jaime as the lad skipped away, relieved of his duty.

"I haven't a clue. I know nothing of magic."

Cary snorted. "That's a crock."

"If you mean I'm lying, I swear I don't know how I'm able to do what it is I do. I'm still not wholly convinced I'm doing anything. When Adrian worked magic I could see it happening. A shimmering, like heat rising from the pavement."

Cary frowned, his eyes all but disappearing beneath his bulky brow. "I don't need to see it to feel it. You saved our lives."

"And for what purpose?" Gazing out over the sea again, Cary didn't reply. By Captain Warner's estimations and his own, they'd make landfall in Boston in a day or two, but the ship was a charter and Jaime knew nothing of what awaited them once they disembarked.

"Has he really never told you where we're going?" he asked without much optimism.

"Dunno why you think he would have," Cary grunted. "He barely credits me with speech."

"Yet he fears you."

"Does he?

"He acts as though he does."

"He fears his master. I'm just the enforcer."

"Whatever you are, keep at it."

Jutting out his chin, his beard bristling, Cary didn't reply. Despite their closeness over the final days at sea, he had resumed his attitude of near hostility now that Jaime was no longer in immediate danger. Jaime had put the matter from his mind as best he could. A pity, for he'd liked thinking of the man as a friend.

They landed at Boston on the eve of the fourth day, as Jaime had predicted. Or guessed, he wasn't sure which, for he'd said it without thinking, that day before the storm. After provisioning the ship they tacked up the coast to Halifax, where Captain Warner was well glad to be rid of his irritating cargo. Not even the cabin boy wished to sign on to the rest of Sandover's mysterious venture, though he was made a handsome offer of not only money but two suits of new clothes and nothing heavier to carry than a valise. Though the crossing had been horrific, it was with surprising reluctance that Jaime bid the crew farewell. Not so surprising given that Cary was now the only thing standing between him and Sandover.

They boarded a cargo steamer, the acrid coal smoke pluming from its stacks damping Jaime's acute sense of smell. Yet as they beat up the vast Gulf of St Lawrence he could feel the change, the mineral sharpness of a great river emptying itself into the briny sea, making his skin tingle with something like anticipation.

Sandover had booked a cabin (though not one for Jaime or Cary) and had remained out of sight for the first few days. He had emerged not the skeletal wretch he'd been by the end of the ocean crossing but his well-groomed self, the salt and other worse stains vanished from his silk suits, his gilded hair lustrous, his sun-wrecked skin once more pale as the moon. Only his eyes showed the lingering damage, wheeling and darting about like flies over a battleground as he sashayed towards Jaime where he stood at the starboard rail.

Far across the silvery gulf lay a dark smear of land, the first they'd seen since passing Cape Breton, and Jaime was struck by a staggering urge to throw himself into the water and take his chances. Except they'd stop the ship and send a rescue party to fish him out, and he'd have served nothing except enraging Sandover and betraying Cary. He gripped the rail as Sandover neared, willing a neutral expression onto his face.

"How fortunate to find you alone, Mr. Skye," Sandover rasped, for his magic had left his voice unhealed. "Your watchdog bares his teeth too eagerly for my liking."

"What is it you want?"

"To uproot the source of our animosity, *cheri*, and cast it aside. I would that we were better friends, Mr. Skye."

"I would rather be better strangers."

Sandover laughed, pursing his painted lips. "Yet we need not be at odds, Mr. Skye. I would make your journey far more pleasant, if only you would do one thing for me." He laid his porcelain-skinned hand on the rail, his fingers splayed, reaching for Jaime's.

Thrusting his hands in his pockets, Jaime stepped back. "Don't touch me."

Sandover's nasty smile tightened. "You misunderstand me, *mon cheri*—"

"I don't think I do. You used me against my will."

"But *cheri*, I would make it so good for you," he purred, advancing with every step Jaime retreated. "Pleasure like nothing you've known. A bliss most sublime. And I'm asking so very nicely."

"Ask all you like, the answer's the same. I don't want you touching me." His heel struck something solid: the capstan, an iron axel standing waist high that served as a winch for heavy cargo. Sandover's sickly scent was all over him, clinging to his skin, the cold metal hard against the backs of his legs, the tang of iron on his tongue, sapping his strength and leaving him helpless as Sandover reached for him...

"Oi!" Cary shouted as he came storming up the deck. "Lay off him, you greasy nightmare."

Sandover pulled back with a hiss. "You cannot evade me forever," he whispered. "I will have my way." He turned to Cary with his usual sneer. "As for you, why aren't you guarding the cargo?"

"What is it I'm guarding anyway?"

"Why should I tell you?"

"So I can decide if I give a damn."

Sandover drew up, his eyes bulging. "You dare defy me?" he rasped. "With all that's at stake?"

"I'll take those odds," Robb replied in the same flat tone. "You're not my master, you greasy fop. You and me answer to the same man and if he finds out you're playing silly beggars with his asset, he'll boil you alive."

Sandover tossed his golden curls. "The duke and I have an alliance."

"Until you stop serving his purposes."

"Enough!" He drew back his hand as if he would strike Robb, who remained unmoved. His face pinched, Sandover lowered his hand. "You will do as you're told, Mr. Robb."

"Or what?"

A flat sheen passed over Sandover's pale eyes as he raised his right hand again. Rather than lash out, he closed his fingers, making a claw. A crushing pain took hold of Jaime's chest, as though Sandover was gripping his lungs and wringing the breath from them. Black oblivion crowded his vision, his heart labouring against the inescapable weight. Just as suddenly the pressure eased, and he roused to find he had fallen to his knees. Robb stood over him, fists clenched, ruin in his eyes.

"Don't tempt me, you ratbag," he growled at Sandover, who had retreated several paces. "If you expect me to see this through, you leave him the hell alone."

"You can't threaten me," Sandover retorted, sneering down his powdered nose. "I hold all the power, Mr Robb. Something you and your beloved would do well to remember." He turned on his satin heel and pranced away, his silk coat swishing.

"Beloved?" Jaime repeated as Cary helped him to his feet. "Does he suspect we're, well..."

"Heaven help the man who does something out of the goodness of his heart," Cary muttered. He stomped off in the opposite direction, towards the hatch that led to the hold. Rather than be left alone, Jaime followed.

At last the gulf began to narrow, until both banks showed as low shadows to port and starboard. They were passing more and more vessels, creeping barges like theirs, sailing ships of every size, fishing vessels bedecked with nets and heavy lines on thick poles. Another few days brought them to the city of Quebec, a French settlement on the rocky northern bank. Though Jaime had hoped they'd go ashore so he might lose himself in a crowd, he changed his mind on hearing that the port was rotten with typhus due to an epidemic sweeping through the Irish refugees crowding the primitive barracks.

He spent the next several days on a circuit between the hold and the deck, both only tolerable for so long. Belowdecks, the thrum and knock of the engines and the stink of grease and coal that stained their churning wake overcame his every sense and left him gasping. Above, he dwelled in a persistent fear, a sickening sense that dreadful things were creeping up on him, if not Sandover then something even worse.

Cary was indifferent, answering in monotone grunts when he answered at all, until Jaime would give up seeking his company and curl up on the heap of canvas he was using as a bed. Each time he woke from a fitful sleep, Cary would be in the same pose, sitting cross-legged atop the smaller of Sandover's crates, his hands loose on his thighs, his face as stony as the riverbanks that rose higher and higher the further they travelled, their summits cloaked in impenetrable forests of evergreens.

Meanwhile Sandover stalked the barge like an overdressed ghost, appearing at the door to the hold without warning to do nothing but stare, or pacing the deck muttering hoarsely to himself. Jaime avoided him as best he could, until he himself felt a spectre, an unreal presence barely noticed by the ordinary world. At least he got served when he lined up with the crew at mealtimes, his face one among many.

He woke one day from a fitful sleep to a new sensation. A subtle warmth whispering across his skin, he unfolded himself slowly from his cramped position on the musty pile of canvas then crept out of the hold. The high banks of the river had fallen away and they traversed a vast plane of freshwater, a lake unlike any Jaime had known. Cary was at the prow, and turned as Jaime approached.

"They say there's bigger ones to come" he grumbled, pointing his chin at the slate-blue water that surrounded them in all directions.

"Bigger lakes than this?" Jaime's toes curled in his boots, as if trying to root him to the deck.

"Some of the deepest on earth."

"Why are we here?"

"You're guess is as good as mine, waterman."

PORT OF CALL

Their first major port of call was the capital Kingston, a charming small city with a number of fine stone buildings. The British garrison of Fort Henry stood on a point overlooking the mouth of the river and the naval dockyards. All of which Cary was forced to surmise from the barge's hold, for Sandover had confined him and Jaime to the vessel rather than risk an escape.

"That's their capital, is it?" he said, stepping back from the porthole. "Not much to it."

"What about your country?" Jaime asked, hopping up to sit on a nearby crate. "Is it anything like this?"

"No. But it's no easier on you white fellas. Probably harder."

"They say it never rains there."

"They?"

"I've read some popular accounts of the Australian colony. It sounds like a dangerous place."

"It's the colonists who make it dangerous."

"You don't mean to tell me it's unpleasant to live under British rule. My, but they're so nice to everyone in the places they conquer."

They put in at a few more towns along the northern shore of the massive lake, more than once unloading the goods into a fishing boat moored alongside, as not every harbour was navigable for the long, heavy barge. As the hold emptied Jaime felt less hemmed in and they spent more of their time here. It was the one place they were sure not to see Sandover, who stalked the deck day and night, speaking to no one but himself.

They had left the port of Oshawa that morning. It was a warmer day than they'd yet had, and the hold was stifling. Cary was on deck, dozing on a stack of crates near the prow, when the captain approached. A long-limbed man with thin lips and sagging skin, he reminded Cary sharply of a frilled lizard, as if he might rear up and run at you if alarmed, flapping his neck and hissing.

"Don't mind me, Mr. Robb," he said as Cary made to get up. "Just marking the cargo for our next port of call."

Some distance ahead along the green shore, a veil of smoke hung above a greyish smear that marked the city of Toronto. Pinned between two rivers, its harbour protected by a largish island, the city clung to the shoreline. Factory stacks rose from the skyline to the west and east, the land rising behind it heavily forested and dotted here and there with clustered buildings that suggested villages.

With the help of a tugboat and much shouting back and forth the barge moored at one of the wooden piers extending from the busy dockyards. Cary stayed where he was, watching the crew offload the cargo down the slanting gangplank. He got to his feet when he saw Sandover leave his cabin and join the captain, who stood near the wheelhouse hatch.

"And when will we arrive at Toronto?" Sandover asked tiredly.

"We just did," replied the captain with a wobble of his chin.

"*Mon Dieu, c'est tout?*" Sandover murmured, his cheeks paling as he gaze mournfully at the bustling dockyard. He startled as a crewman appeared behind him, a coiled rope in his arms.

"Sorry, Mr. Sandover, but could you please step aside?" the captain said. As the crewman passed Sandover gave him a simpering smile. He startled again as another fellow came from the other direction bearing a long-handled gaff.

"Sorry, sir, just need to get by you there."

Tossing his head, Sandover stomped a silken heel. "I shall be in my cabin packing my personal belongings. You may inform me when my cargo is unloaded."

"I've sent the cabin boy to help you," the captain said as Sandover started for his cabin. "He ought to be in there right now."

Sandover wheeled about, colour draining from his cheeks. "You let him—oh *mon Dieu*!" Sputtering in French, Sandover bolted for the cabin. Before he reached it the door was flung open and the cabin boy, a gangly lad whose face was more freckle than not, came reeling out, wheezing and batting at the noxious cloud that followed him. As he fell to his knees, clutching his throat, Sandover hissed a bitter word. The livid cloud coalesced into a shining droplet then winked out of being.

The cabin boy's face was a violent purple, his eyes wheeling as he thrashed back and forth. Sandover made a plucking motion towards him in the air and said another strange word. With a great gulp of air the boy lurched forward then collapsed on the deck where he lay gasping.

"Let this teach you to ask permission before handling a man's possessions," Sandover said, stepping over his quaking form. He entered the cabin and slammed the door.

Briefly, very briefly, Cary pondered the outcome of setting the ship on fire and making sure Sandover stayed on it. Many lives endangered, much damage done, and possibly no outcome aside from enraging a madman who could flatten the dockyard with a wave of his hand. Swallowing his useless anger, he joined Jaime where he lingered near the top of the gangway, gazing out over the hurly burly of the dockyard.

"Don't even think about it," Cary said under his breath as Jaime tensed.

"Think about what?"

"Running off."

Still looking elsewhere, Jaime leaned closer and spoke from the side of his mouth. "This is our best chance. He's out of sight, and no one here knows us from Adam."

"I can't."

Jaime turned and glared up at him. "What does Sandover have over you?"

"Never you mind."

"It's standing between us and freedom."

"Let's find out first what he wants you for."

Jaime's taut expression softened and he leaned against Cary to speak in a whisper. "We'll never have this chance again. Come away with me, now. Please, Cary, I can't—" With a gasp he broke off and stepped back a few paces as Sandover emerged from his cabin.

"I'm sorry," Cary murmured.

"I don't need your apologies. I need your help." Before Cary replied Jaime turned and stomped down the gangplank.

"Well?" Sandover called across the deck. "Get after him."

His mouth clamped shut to keep from telling Sandover off mightily, his insides churning with guilt, Cary followed Jaime ashore. The timber-sided warehouses in the busy little port were all very new save for one old hall weathered silver by the years. The ground was a silty stew of mud and gravel and horse-dung that emitted a lively fragrance in the noonday sun. Wooden plank footpaths lined the unpaved street beyond, ridged with deep ruts from the wheels of countless wagons.

"This must be a nightmare when it rains," Jaime said, as a man crossing the street caught his toe in a rut and went sprawling. Sandover had caught up to them and now stopped at the corner to consult a small leather-bound book, his coat of embroidered sea-green silk and tricorn hat with matching plume attracting the curious eye of every passer-by.

"Will you tell us where we're going?" Jaime asked as Sandover slapped the book closed.

"To speak with someone who will explain our purpose, my dear Mr. Skye." Sandover gave one of his obnoxious bows then started westward, the planks ringing hollowly under his heeled slippers.

"Does it worry you that he's being so polite?" said Jaime as they followed.

STRIKE & ECKHART

Having only been amalgamated as a city in the prior decade, Toronto had neither a public omnibus nor hackneys to be hired, and to Sandover's irritation they were obliged to travel the whole distance on foot. They ended in an industrial district just east of the lunatic asylum. Here he led them through a warren of workshops and manufactories to a squat brick building tucked between a carpet-maker and a reeking smithy. A soot-tarnished sign over the broad swinging doors read *Strike & Eckhart, Electrical Manufactory*. A man in a stained suit of heavy canvas emerged from the left-hand door which stood open. He raised his dark-lensed glasses to reveal a startling patch of pale skin blazing across the upper left of his otherwise deeply brown face.

"Can I help you?" he asked in a softly twanging accent.

"Is your master about?" Sandover said, sounding bored.

The man looked him up and down with a flick of his eyes then glanced at the others. "What is it you want?" he said in a harder tone.

"I told you. Now go and fetch him, boy."

Yanking off his heavy leather gloves, the man laughed deep in his chest, though he wasn't smiling. "You must be new around here. You better tell me what you want before I get sick of asking."

"Hello!" Another face poked around the door, this one pink and topped with a wave of sandy blond hair. He was wearing a similar pair of dark glasses which he removed as he approached, grinning broadly. "May I help you?"

"I do hope so," Sandover said with a strained smile. "Hercule Lorraine de la Croix Sandover, Lord Magister and Inheritor of—"

"Ah yes, Mr. Sandover!" the tall man interrupted, snatching up Sandover's limp hand and shaking it vigorously as Sandover's eyes twitched with suppressed feeling. "How good to finally meet you. I see you've met my partner Mr. Strike."

"Not exactly," Cary said. He stepped around Sandover and put out his hand. "Good to meet you. Name's Robb." Strike hesitated, then met his handshake. "And I'll assume this is Mr. Eckhart," Cary said, nodding to the other man.

"Norton Eckhart, PhD, very much at your service." Beaming, Eckhart pumped Robb's hand, then Jaime's. "Well, don't stand on ceremony," he went on as he ushered them towards the workshop, oblivious to Sandover's growing impatience. "Come in, come in, I'll see if we have seats for you all. Though you, my good man, might exceed our rickety old chairs' tolerances," he said, grinning at Cary.

"We don't intend to take much of your time, Doctor Eckhart," Sandover said tersely. "Tell us what you know and we'll leave you be."

"Oh. I was going to put the kettle on just now so you're welcome to stay and—"

Strike cleared his throat. Eckhart glanced at him, his fair cheeks flushing. "I suppose we are in the middle of something. Oh well, next time."

He led them into what looked like a machinist's shop, then through a door and along a hall with flowered paper on the walls that seemed to be part of a home, then out a door at the far end which led to another rough workshop. Wooden lockers lined the brick walls and a cabinet of wide but very short drawers stood under the single broad window at the far end. In the centre stood a large table with a stone top.

"By god, what's that smell?" Jaime muttered, for the room had an underlying stink different from both the dockyard muck and the acrid industrial smoke billowing from the local factories. A rank, aldehydic scent of rotting flesh and vegetation like the leavings of a flood.

"You're lucky to have arrived when you did," Eckhart said. "I've recently obtained a specimen—"

"Specimen?" Sandover cried, looking about urgently.

"I assure you it's entirely dead," Eckhart said with a wan smile. "And a bit ripe. I'm still looking for a vessel large enough to preserve it in. Here, have a look." He took a large folder from the top drawer of the cabinet and passed it to Jaime.

With reluctance he opened it to find several drawings. The first showed a long, fleshy tubule, not an octopus' arm or the stem of a plant but something in between, with a regular series of nubs along one side and a flat, fleshy appendage at the end. "How big is this thing?" he breathed, his skin prickling with horror.

"There's a scale to one side. I believe it's around twenty feet long, give or take."

"Show it to me," Sandover barked, snatching the page from Jaime's hand and revealing the page underneath, a detailed illustration of the strange appendage, the pucker in its centre reminding him of a lamprey's sucking mouth.

"It appears to reproduce very easily," Eckhart said, as he fussed with the latch of the large trunk standing beside the cabinet. "Cut off one of his limbs and a dozen more will spawn from the segments. That's when it spreads most easily, in its, er, larval form. Might you give me a hand?" he said to Cary. He threw open the lid of the trunk, the stink bludgeoning Jaime's nose and churning his stomach.

Fighting a violent nausea, he threw his arm over his face. "I don't want to know what's in there."

"*Plus courage*, Mr. Skye," Sandover mumbled through the lacy handkerchief covering his nose as Cary and Eckhart wrestled the heavy bundle of damp canvas out of the trunk and onto the table. "Remember, this one's dead."

"*This* one?"

"There does appear to be a nest of them," Eckhart said in the pinched voice of someone trying not to breathe. He threw back the last flap of canvas and made a gruesome face. "Blast. It's really starting to rot."

It was a section of tentacle. The same as in the illustration, segmented like an earthworm, with pale, saucer-sized nodules covering the underside. Both ends were badly damaged, as if hacked by blunt swords. A viscous greenish liquid was seeping from the ragged wounds. All told it was a good twelve inches across and twice that in length. Any animal that could bear such a large appendage would be enormous. Was he meant to catch this creature? Extract it from its underwater nest and tame it?

"Seems to have had a run-in with a steamboat's propeller," Eckhart said, fanning the air in front of his face. "A larger section washed up ashore the next day."

"And if one were to attempt to capture such a beast?" Sandover asked, circling the table to inspect it.

"I can't see how," Eckhart said with a dry chuckle. As if the very thought was ludicrous.

"Any animal can be taken by a savvy hunter," Sandover replied. He licked his lips and Eckhart's smile fell away.

"You can't possibly mean that. You described yourself as a man of science, not a trophy seeker."

"And your science brings you no accolades?"

Eckhart's spine stiffened, his whole demeanour hardening. "This isn't research, it's a damned safari, isn't it? I'll have no part of this." He began wrapping the ghastly thing in its stained canvas.

"But my dear Doctor Eckhart," Sandover said, baring his teeth in the mockery of a smile. "We would pay you handsomely for your cooperation."

"You shan't have it at any cost," Eckhart retorted. "I'm sorry but you need to leave."

"Don't be a fool!" Sandover hissed, that lizard flatness sheathing his eyes as he closed the distance between them. "Do you think I can't simply take what I want? Command you as easily as I do these miserable puppets?"

Fear in his eyes, Eckhart stepped back, colliding with the cabinet. Cary growled, his hands tensing to fists, but before anyone could act there was a motion in the doorway.

"Get the hell away from him!" Strike stood at the doorway, He advanced into the room, light gathering around his hands, a strange power radiating from his skin. "I said back off, Frenchie."

Sandover made a careless gesture over his shoulder and Strike grunted, slumping forward like he'd been punched in the stomach.

"That's it, I've had enough of your shit," he snarled. As he raised his fists they seemed to catch fire, a blue-white haze that crackled in the murky air. "Either you get out or I'm throwing you out."

"Emory, be careful," Eckhart cried as Sandover whirled to face him, his hands poised.

"He doesn't scare me," Strike growled.

"You'll bring the house down on our heads!"

"Don't tempt me," Sandover spat. "Indeed, I ought to burn your pathetic city to the ground to prove its uselessness."

"Do so, and I'll hunt you to the end of the earth," Strike snarled, the blue-white flames dancing up and down his arms. "Now get out before I lose my temper, and don't even think about coming back."

"I'll get what I want, my dear doctor," Sandover said, turning his back on Strike as if he was part of the furniture. "With or without you. And don't expect me to be merciful once I do."

SMALL MERCIES

As Sandover marched from the room, Eckhart and his part-ner Strike wrapped the appalling thing in its reeking canvas. Jaime was still as stone, once again covering his nose and mouth.

The others were arguing softly, Eckhart's fair face red with emotion, Strike curtailing a series of angry gestures towards the door, the ozone scent of his power burning through the stench. If ever there was someone who might help them, it was these men. A thought not lost on Jaime, as he swallowed hard, wiping his damp cheeks on his sleeve.

"Please," he said, his voice cracking. "Please, will you help us?"

"Not for anything, you butchers," Eckhart spat, his chest swelling.

"It's not like you think. We're not here by choice, Mr. Robb and I. He's being blackmailed and I was abducted." Strike's whole body stiffened as Eckhart gasped, covering his mouth.

"We're your best, maybe your only chance to stop Sandover from harming this creature," Jaime went on. "Can you help us stay alive long enough to try?"

The other men shared a look, long and full of feeling. Then Strike nodded, a single sharp jerk of his head. "Right then," Eckhart replied with a weak smile. "Let's see what we can do for you."

While Strike left the room to retrieve something, Eckhart took a large hardbound book from a shelf by the door and opened it on the top of the cabinet. "Here's where the specimen was found, on the southern shore of Manitoulin Island," he said, pointing in the gazetteer at the large landmass that dominated the north of the great broken hand of water known as Lake Huron. "The steamboat was badly damaged in the encounter, though the official word being put around is that the vessel ran aground on one of the little limestone islands that litter the shoreline."

"No one knows about this?" Cary asked as Jaime bent over the map to inspect it.

"It was a cargo vessel," Eckhart replied. "And it happened on a foggy morning so eye-witnesses are few. The lake is becoming a busy shipping route as it's by far the easiest way into both the interior of the Dominion and the Wisconsin Territory. The last thing our governor wants is a mass panic that ships are at risk of attack by...well, whatever this is."

This sobering thought silenced them until Strike returned. "This will stay lit in all weather," he said, sliding back the lid on a small tin box to reveal a smouldering coal, its ruddy heat gleaming from within its cocoon of white ash. "Blow on it like any cinder and it will give you fire enough to start most any kindling."

"Or a candle?" Robb said, nodding at the half-burned tallow Eckhart was holding.

"It's a lodestone wick," Strike replied. "The flame points northward."

"We do have a compass," Jaime said as Cary stowed the small box and the candle in the leather satchel where he kept his tobacco and other goods.

"Which will be so useful in the dark, won't it?" Strike replied evenly.

"Ah. True."

"Thanks for deciding to help us," Cary said as they started for the door.

"I only hope we've been of use," Eckhart replied.

"We'll take any help we can get."

"Then by all means take this too," said Strike. He opened a cupboard behind him and retrieved a squat brown apothecary's jar, a pungent herbal aroma seeping from under the hinged lid.

"Is this some kind of magic potion?" Jaime asked.

"It's to keep away the flies," Strike replied with a grimace.

"Which flies?"

He swapped glances with Eckhart. "You'll know when you find them."

"Bloody hell," Cary muttered as he tucked the jar away with the other enchanted goods. "I hate flies."

They spent several days in Toronto as Sandover sought passage northward. Plenty of ships plied the long route through Lake St Clair and its river to Lake Huron and beyond, westward through Lake Superior to the trading post of Fond du Lac, at the very heart of the vast continent. Sandover wished to travel overland, a distance on the map of far fewer miles. He would not answer why, not to Jaime or Cary, nor to any of the agents of the various transport companies who came calling, none of whom took Sandover's admittedly lucrative offer.

"It's not a matter of distance," said the skimble-shanked company man as he rolled up his charts. "There is no better way to get where you're going than by water."

"I've had quite enough of water, Mr. Turnbull," Sandover said through his teeth.

"But a load of that weight?" Turnbull said with a note of frustration. "There's not a vehicle in my fleet I'd risk on the roads available. I'm very sorry that you expect us to have Old World comforts, Mr—I meant, Lord Sandover, but here we make do. Good day, and to you gentlemen as well."

Cary went to open the door for Turnbull. Sandover remained in his chair, drumming his fingers on the armrests as he gazed into the unlit hearth.

"I don't know what that fellow expects when he won't even disclose the contents of the cargo," Turnbull said as he stepped into the hall. "What's his objection to shipping?"

"We were trapped in the doldrums on our Atlantic passage. Maybe he holds a grudge."

"Well you can be sure of no doldrums on the Lakes, Mr. Robb. Quite the opposite. If you're in open water and the clouds turn, get to safe harbour if you at all can."

When Cary returned, Sandover had gone into his bedroom. To sulk, to preen, to write in his weird little book. To come storming out without warning to haul them across town to another unwilling transport firm's office.

Jaime was by the window looking out over the street. In anticipation of the cruelties to come Cary had done his best to stay aloof from the other man. They spoke little, and then only of dull practicalities like the need for fresh towels or whether they might order more tea. It had rained this morning and the unpaved street resembled a silty river bottom, every passing horse's legs coated with mud to the fetlock, every man's boots or trousers to the knee. Regardless, Cary would have happily gotten filthy head to toe if it meant a chance to leave the hotel room.

"Do you think his highness trusts you to take me for a walk?" Jaime asked, letting the curtain fall closed.

"Don't bloody care," Cary grunted. "We're going whether he does or not, or I'm going to go round the bend. Get your hat."

SHAME

They went where the planked walks took them, Jaime skipping across the muddy intersections while Cary plodded through, stopping now and then to stomp the mud off his boots. It was otherwise a pleasant enough town, with tidy rows of new brick buildings lining the broad if messy streets. By his sheer bulk Cary attracted several odd looks, making Jaime feel pleasantly inconspicuous.

After a mile or so they entered a tidy residential block, where a row of newly built town-homes faced a treed square with a small ornamental pond at the far end. A pretty young woman in a muslin dress and bright pink wrapper sat on a bench by the pond with her nose in a book. Beside her, a much older and plainer woman was bent over some needlework.

The young woman eyes flew open as she caught sight of them over the edge of her book. Her stillness alerted her guardian, who stuffed her bit of embroidery into a tapestry bag then hurried the young woman from the park with several backward glances.

"That was rude," Cary said.

"Do we look all that dreadful?" Jaime bent over the pond to see his reflection, but the persistent breeze ruffled the surface. When he looked up Cary was nowhere to be seen. Jaime spun about, the prickling fear dying away as he spied Cary sitting with his back to a tree on the turf beyond the fountain.

It was a warm day and the park was very quiet, save for the odd birdcall and the faint sound of a pianoforte drifting from one of the houses facing the square. Cary's head was sagging, his chin on his chest, as if he'd fallen asleep. Sitting on the bench the women had abandoned, Jaime watched for several minutes more, weighing his chances if he were to simply walk away. He hadn't any money, and aside from Cary he had no friends, unless he counted Eckhart and Strike. He was all alone in a far-away country that was mainly untrammelled wilderness, without even a stout coat to survive the winters that the dominion's people described with such a mix of hate and admiration. *You'll want to be strong to make it here*, he had heard more than once, and Jaime was anything but.

If he only had more knowledge of how to use his powers. He had put no effort into learning while on the voyage, mainly to frustrate Sandover. But if he wanted to defeat the mage, he needed more control.

When he was a child it had been so easy. Barely a matter of thought, more of desire, to make the little droplets jump from the surface. *Plip*, he had called the aimless game, first played in secret in grimy puddles in the lane behind his foster home. Then one fateful night in the bath. His foster father's rage had surpassed any of his previous fits, and Jaime had slept that night on the boards of his bed, his mattress having been removed as punishment for telling lies.

Would he have suffered less if they had known the truth? If he had grown up understanding that others' ignorance was the lie? If he'd grown up knowing Adrian, who might have mentored him, who had said he would have raised Jaime as his own son if only he'd known.

Yet another question, for Jaime's birth father had shared his elemental abilities, and yet he and Jaime's mother had died at sea.

Barely more than an infant, Jaime had been sent to fosterage with an Ordinary family in England, away from his home and his only blood relative, herself said to be a witch of astonishing prowess. More questions than answers, and no one to ask.

Standing at the low sandstone wall bordering the pond, he looked across the gently rippled surface. Adrian had brought him to a similar place on the day they met, though the glory of Kensington Gardens was to this dusty little square as St Peters Basilica to a country parsonage. That day Jaime had denied having any power at all, so stridently that his unchecked emotions had churned the pond to whitecaps and caused a rainstorm without him believing that he'd done either.

Less than a month later, he still barely understood his abilities, but it couldn't be true that every time he'd put in whole-hearted effort to work water that the change had come by happenstance. He had *felt* the ocean move to meet his will. Felt the calling of the storm, its wordless promise of oblivion. Had felt its grip loosen as he'd steered the ship like a man born to the sailor's life, though before that journey he'd never set foot on a vessel larger than a Thames punt.

With a last look about for observers, he scooped up a handful of water. A puddle the size of a sovereign, it lay in the valley of his palm, a tiny ripple shivering across its surface in echo of his heartbeat.

Up...

He leapt back as the spoonful of water in his hand formed itself into a shimmering globe and jumped two inches in the air. The fat drop shattered on the edge of his hand, wetting his sleeve and leaving a dark blot on the warm sandstone that began to dry as soon as it landed.

Biting back tears for all the years he'd lost to self-doubt and torment, he faced the pond and reached out his hands. *Up...*

And as he thought this he threw his hands to the sky, expecting nothing but to look like a fool. Instead the pond erupted, as had the pond in Kensington that first day, two great spouts of water arcing across the surface. A thrilling glee coursed through him, not the awkward tremor of sensual release but simply joy as the scintillating drops rained down on the shining surface of the water.

He did it again but more gently, marvelling at the twin swells that rose and fell in concert with rise and fall of his hands. Curious to test his limits, he envisioned the pond quiet once more, communicating his desire with a gentle motion of his hand, as though stroking the fur of some tameable beast, until the water was as still as glass.

To imagine the mechanism, the physical force he had miraculously harnessed, was to damage the miracle, ask too much too soon. Better to let the facts speak for themselves, as with a casual flicking gesture he caused the water's surface to erupt in another curving wake.

As the haze of droplets cleared he saw Cary standing on the far side of the pond. A tremor of fear ran through him as the other man circled the pond. So many times, such joys as these had led to a nightmare. To cold, crowded wards and the torments within as doctor after doctor attempted in ignorance to cure him of being himself. Of being Jaime Skye, the Inheritor of the Northwest, the Defender of Angels, or so Adrian had called him.

This wasn't madness but power. A power beyond ordinary understanding. He was the bearer of this power.

And he would never be ashamed again.

NEED

Jaime was afraid of him, trembling as he glared at Cary through the falling spray, his face pale behind the gingery freckles earned on their sea voyage. Yet he stood firm, his back stiff, gaze unyielding. A man who knew he was beaten but wasn't prepared to stop fighting. Cary had hated those jobs, when the only choice was to club the runaway prisoner into unconsciousness and drag him back to the lock-up.

"Has Sandover seen you do that?" he asked.

"I hope not," Jaime replied, visibly relaxing. "I didn't wake you, did I?"

"No worries. We ought to get back soon, anyway."

"I used to cause myself no end of trouble over it," Jaime said, falling into step beside him. "At first, I got whipped. When that didn't work they sent me to a hospital."

"They thought you were sick?"

"I wasn't sick, I was troublesome. I should have said *asylum*."

"God's truth."

"I was never sick, I realize now," Jaime said with a crooked smile. "But I was so young I couldn't help but take them at their word. The doctors, my foster family. They all told me it was for my own good. That I couldn't possibly have done what they saw me do. Make a rainbow, make water jump from a bucket. Such little things." He swallowed hard, thrusting his hands deep in his pockets

"Most people don't understand what we do."

"At least you have strength on your side," he said with another brief smile. "I can't imagine anyone persuading you into something you didn't want to do."

If only strength was enough. "Is it true you can't drown?" Cary asked as they passed through the park gates.

"So far as I know," he replied, kicking at gravel. "I did try to once, when I'd had enough of everything. Walked into the sea with my pockets full of rocks, sat down on the bottom and waited to run out of breath."

Behind his back Cary made a sign of warding. "And?" he grunted.

He spread his hands with a sad little laugh. "And here I am. I might still be down there if that fisherman's trawl line hadn't hooked on my shirt."

"What about your family?"

He shrugged casually, though his voice wavered. "I haven't any. Or at least none who acknowledge me. My parents died while I was an infant, and my foster family turned me out when I was not quite thirteen. My friend Adrian said my grandmother is still alive, but I'll believe that when I see it. *If* I see it. Faith, we're going die over here, aren't we?"

"As long as I take that devil with me."

When they reached the hotel, they endured several minutes of San-dover's complaints, but he had nothing much to complain about and soon retreated to his room. Cary was tempted to do the same. Unlike aboard the barge, Sandover had booked a suite with rooms for each of them, but something in the lift of Jaime's chin and the set of his shoulders as he resumed his post at the window plucked the strings of Cary's intuition.

Not for the first time he wondered if Jaime knew that he'd become part of Cary's dreamings. He'd not said a thing about it, for the dreams were terrifying, mainly to do with him murdering Jaime by any number of dreadful means, from poison to fire to tearing him limb from limb. Hideous visions which rose now and then in his waking hours to remind him of his role in this nightmare adventure. Worse than his dreams about harming Jaime were the nights when he walked with the duke, tracking him through an endless nightmare landscape of sucking mud and agony, or fleeing from him through the same. True sendings, for he had woken from each with black earth on his tongue.

The more fully that Jaime came into his power, the greater the chance of him escaping, and the harder Cary's job became. The thing was to keep Jaime believing they were friends, even though it could never be so. Keep him close, keep him safe, so he'd do what was asked of him.

A spindled table and two chairs stood near the window and Cary sat cautiously, the chair creaking beneath his bulk. "How long were you in the asylum?" he asked. "If you don't mind me asking."

"Which visit?" Jaime said dryly, not turning from the window. "I ought to do the calculation, find out how many weeks of my life were stolen from me."

"You get locked up a lot?"

"I did. I should think I'm past it, now that I know the truth." He let the curtain fall and sat down across from Cary. "And you? Have you always known that you had power?"

"The aunties made sure I knew."

"You have a big family?"

"They're not that kind of auntie." More a flock of stickybeaks, but Jaime nodded in understanding.

"Every village has a few of those," he said kindly. "My landlady Mrs. Meldrum was exceedingly interested in my activities." He sat up abruptly, his mild expression giving way to fear. "I hope no one's harmed her. What if they went to her first? I swear, if I ever find this duke of his—"

"Don't bother. I know the thirst for vengeance but don't seek it against that devil."

"He doesn't frighten me."

"He should. I tell you, I could turn Sandover inside out. Set him alight and make him burn. But I won't. I need him. I need him alive."

"Tell me why."

"No."

Jaime gazed at him, the seconds spooling out, counted by the brass clock on the mantel, the hammer of Cary's heart. "So that was a lie, was it? When you said we'd sort ourselves out on dry land. Do you remember?"

"Yes."

"You said we were the strongest thing going. What happened to that?"

"I wasn't lying."

"Yet here we still are."

Cary didn't reply. Why did it matter if this miserable man respected him, as long as he obeyed? Cary had done it hard for years, been the master of himself, surrendering any aims of love or friendship to the work of staying alive. Yet as Jaime looked away he felt a pang of loss strike through him. Without a word Jaime rose from the table and went into his room and left Cary to feel it alone.

The weather was criminal for the rest of the week, bringing first a windstorm then days of blatting rain. Jaime stayed in his room as much as possible and otherwise kept his head down, never looking Cary in the eye if he could help it. A subtle and ruinous sign of how deeply Cary had wounded him.

At last a clear day dawned. Sandover had hired a band of Iroquois to guide them northwest, and they met in the courtyard of the hotel to discuss the terms. Though they were dressed in settlers' garb of plain buckskin trousers and cloth coats, their firm stature and firmer faces were enough to stand them apart from the other people milling about or passing the courtyard's open arch.

The Iroquois' representative was a handsome, broadly-built man in a flat-brimmed felt hat, who went by the ill-fitting name Little George. "Sure we can take you overland," he said once Sandover had explained the route.

"I'm pleased to find someone who appreciates my preferences," Sandover purred as he folded away his map.

"It's your money, Lord Sandover," Little George said. "We'll take as long as you want to take."

"It's not a matter of time, friend," Sandover said with a false smile. "I have a particular need to avoid the lakes."

"So you say."

"Yes. And as to that, I must ask how you will be transporting the cargo."

"We won't be."

Sandover's ugly smile died. "Pardon?"

"The cargo is up to you, Lord Sandover. We were hired to guide you. Not to fetch and carry."

"What am I meant to do?"

"You could try carrying it yourself," George said mildly.

"The largest item weighs two hundred pounds!"

"Then that's going to be mighty heavy. Might want to hire some men to help you."

"But I did," Sandover fairly shrieked. "I hired...*merde*." He snatched his hat off his head to fan himself.

"Hey now, mind your tongue," Little George said, his eyes darkening. "There's no need for rude language."

"I respectfully disagree."

"Now what, your lordship?" Jaime asked with more than a little sarcasm when the guides had gone.

"I'll be damned if I'm going by water," Sandover hissed. "You saw that *thing* at the doctor's. If there are more, I want to have as little do with them as possible."

"So why are we going after it?"

"Because I have accepted my duty, Mr. Skye," Sandover replied with brittle clarity. "Unlike some of us."

"He's blackmailing you too, isn't he?" Cary said.

Sandover turned on him with a snarl, his eyes bulging, two small patches of red blooming on his porcelain cheeks. "I shall ignore the indignity of that question, Mr. Robb." He whirled about and marched up the front steps and into the hotel, his yellow coattails flapping.

"That would be a *yes*," Jaime said quietly.

"Forget him. I'll get us a crew."

"Who do you know here?"

"No worries. I know how to find men."

LES BOYS

Alone in his hotel room, Jaime was practicing. Not merely with water but with his mind, seeking some measure of stillness amid the churning froth of thoughts and emotions. Most of Jaime's magic, he had done by accident. His greatest workings had been performed in a state of mortal panic, when failure had meant his death. Playing with droplets and praying to the sea were all very well, but if he was to confront a nest of sea (yes, fine, *lake*) serpents, he ought to have a greater command of his talents.

And so he had been practicing all week, staying in his room both to avoid Cary and his hot and cold moods and to keep Sandover from watching as his skills advanced. Water-gathering was once an involuntary reflex, the moisture bursting from his skin like sweat whenever his emotions got too heated. With Adrian's help he had learned to fetch water from the air with focused intention. Now he could do so in ready abundance, scoop up handfuls of invisible vapour and fill a glass with the resulting water in under a minute, though not quite with Adrian's finesse.

He sat on the edge of his bed facing the window which he'd opened to let in the humidity. An empty tumbler stood on the nightstand, placed between him and the window. Adrian had said that powers such as theirs depended on mental acuity, on the ability to ignore all distractions and focus the will solely on one's objective. Gazing at the glass, he allowed the noise of horses and wheels and hammering metal drifting through the open window to merge into a single blurry sound, one with the murmuring of voices from the outer room. The glass was empty. He pictured it full. Allowed his unordinary awareness to see it brimming with water. *This,* he thought, as if his thoughts could be heard and the water could hear him. *I want this.*

The lace at the window lifted in the humid wind. The air had cooled, the end of Jaime's nose tingling like it did on a winter's day. Facts he acknowledged then let fall away as he focused his will on the tumbler, the inside of which had begun to cloud. As he watched, a tiny droplet grew, gathering more and more water until the weight of it dragged it down the glass. It joined the puddle of its fellows at the bottom, Jaime's mind so fixed on the one that he hadn't noticed the other droplets form.

Success of a sort and enough for today, and he covered his strained eyes with his hands and let the vision fade. He rose at a knock on the door. Cary, for Sandover never knocked. Jaime cracked opened the door and spoke through the gap. "What do you want?"

"You ought to come downstairs," Cary grunted, glaring at his shoes. "Meet the crew."

"Why do you need me?"

His expression didn't change, but the pause before he replied made Jaime regret his curt words. "It's for your benefit to know what you're working with," he said. "Plus Sandover's going to hate them on sight."

"How so?"

"Think about it. Who'd be cracked enough to take on this job?"

A chance to watch Sandover squirm... "I'll be right with you."

Cracked was a generous understatement. The trio waiting in the courtyard looked half-made, the tallest missing a pinkie finger, the shortest fellow so wall-eyed one couldn't be sure where he was looking even if one stood right in front of him. The one on the end said nothing, lurking behind a curtain of dark hair as his eyes darted about, lighting on every detail. Other than the tall fellow, whose grey satin coat though filthy rivalled Sandover's yellow silk for pointless flamboyance, they were dressed as the Iroquois guides had been, in buckskin and flannel sack jackets.

"Is this *les gars* we're porting?" the tall one asked his mates from the side of his mouth.

"The what?" Sandover spat. As Cary had suggested, the mage was horrified, his mouth in a permanent grimace.

"Don' mind Patrice," said the wall-eyed chap, stepping forward. "He going to say what he likes. You want answers, you come to me. I been all over this here place," he said, gesturing around him, presumably at the country at large and not merely the courtyard. "I know the ways and where to go and no foolin'. But don't listen to Patrice."

"He's not wrong," Patrice said quite happily, clapping his friend on the back. "But don't you worry. We haven't lost anyone in months. Years, even."

"Years, it's been. Isn't that right, boys?" Wall-eye called out to the clutch of equally scruffy men lingering by the arch, earning a chorus of *aye* and *oui* and *d'accord*.

"Can you assure me that you can manage the cargo?" Sandover said in a flat, commanding tone.

"Cargo's no problem, right boys?" Wall-eye replied. "We can take it up the street."

"Yes, but I need to reach Georgian Bay," Sandover said tersely over the others' rising chatter.

"Yep, and that's how we'll get her done, Mr, I mean Lord Sandburger."

"Sandover."

The wall-eyed man blinked twice, neither of his eyes pointing at the mage. "Send over what?"

"My name," Sandover gritted through clenched teeth.

"What for would he send over your name?" asked Patrice. "Did you forget it?"

"No! I...*merde!*" Sandover rounded on Cary, fire in his eyes. "You cannot expect me to tolerate these imbeciles, Mr. Robb."

"I can so. And given you've pissed off every other transport company in town, I expect that you will."

"You don't worry, Mr. Lord Sir," Patrice said with a gappy grin, slapping Sandover on the back. "We'll get her done. I meant get you up Yonge Street. Gets us all the way to Lake Simcoe and then..." He made a gliding motion with his hand. "Straight up to the Bay, licky-slicky."

As Sandover groaned, covering his eyes, Cary flashed Jaime a smile. Jaime made no reply, unsure if watching Sandover suffer was worth the risk of putting their lives in these men's hands. The third fellow hadn't spoken, but nodded when Jaime caught his eye, saluting him with the dented flask he'd been nursing throughout. Madmen, drunks, mages, mutes: fine company for hunting a monster.

YONGE STREET

The boys (les boys, by their own naming) had called it a street, but the northbound road was a raw, rutted trail that would be a mudslide on a rainy day. Sandover had tried to ride on the wagon with the crates but gave up after half an hour of having his bones shaken out of his body. Cary relished the ratbag's discomfort, his feet growing lighter with the mage's every complaint, every baleful glance, every time Sandover had to stop to take a stone out of his fancy shoes then run to catch up with the creaking wagon and its undeclared cargo.

Fair recompense for his persistent sense of being caged in, as they traded the smoke and steel of the city for this narrow cut through the dense forest. Every hill they crested revealed another, taller hill covered in yet more trees, the road a single ribbon of ruddy brown against the endless green. There were many such hills, and despite his talents Sandover was panting and covered in dust by the time they stopped for lunch in the busy village of Newmarket.

They parked in the shade of a row of oaks planted along the edge of the village square. Loaded wagons similar to theirs trundled up and down the road, a steady stream of people passing through the doors of the trading hall and the other brokerages: farmers, hunters, back-country men in fringed buckskin jackets, buyers for city greengrocers in their dusty frock coats, here for the produce grown in the rich soils of the Holland Marsh.

Sandover had vanished as soon as they stopped, as had Patrice and his silent friend Cesar. The wall-eyed chap, who went by Gordo, had laid down on the grass of the square and was now snoring like a rip-saw. The two others in their crew—Coyne, a stringy Devon-born fellow, and Tench, also an Englishman but from the bang opposite end, hailing from Lindisfarne—followed Gordo's lead and had soon added their notes to the honking chorus.

Cary joined Jaime where he sat on the tail of the wagon. "There's a tannery here," Jaime mused, lifting his nose.

"Is that what I can smell?" Cary asked, for the air had a rank pungency.

"That and the herd of pigs someone's driving to town."

"I don't see any—ah." For now he could hear it, the stomp of many little feet and the odd squeal. " Any other hidden talents?" he asked.

"You knew about that," Jaime murmured, kicking his dangling feet.

"Not really. I don't know much about you at all."

Jaime didn't answer, his lips twitching. It was for the best, really, that they not pretend at friendship, not when Cary had to be pre-pared at any minute to treat him like the prisoner he was.

Sandover returned shortly, having magicked the dirt from his clothes. Cesar and Patrice came back just after, Patrice with an im-pressive bruise on his cheek and his satin coat missing a sleeve. "You should have seen the other gens," he said to Gordo.

"Gah, Patrice, that's not the point," Gordo fumed, prodding his friend's naked shoulder. "Why did you not stop him?" he said to

Cesar, who merely shrugged, uncapping his battered flask for another swig.

"Don't be hard on him," Patrice scolded, throwing his bare arm round Cesar's shoulders. "As if he can stop me."

"*Entre nous*," Gordo said more quietly, "should we be getting out of here quick on account of whatever you two arseholes did?"

"Hey boys, get up," Patrice called to the crew. "Let's get her going."

They had reached a plateau and the road no longer climbed so steeply. To keep things interesting, it began to rain. Sandover had grumbled about the expense of having such a large crew, but as the cart's wheels began to sink into the softened road surface the whole gang were needed to unstick it. Cary did not offer to help, reasoning that his duty lay in keeping an eye on Jaime, who had conjured a protection from the rain, a hazy field of irregular light that clung to his skin and clothes, the water beading as if trickling over glass. Sandover as well, though he was making more of a fuss, steaming the water so that he walked in a boiling cloud of vapour lit a soft rose by his pink suit.

Everyone else got wet, including Cary. A working like that used you up if you did it too long. He was no stranger to discomfort, to long, boring marches through unknown territory with a promise of danger at the end. Already Sandover's warding was losing its intensity, the plume on his tricorn draggled and damp, his face rigid with effort. Jaime remained dry somewhat longer, but by evening-time he was squelching in his boots.

Gordo and one of the lesser crew members made a deal with a farmer for the use of his barn for the night. Sandover returned from the stone farmhouse shortly after them with a churlish expression.

"I thought your lordship was gonna bunk at the big house," Patrice asked him over the back of the horse he was currying. "They not have fancy enough a bed for you?"

"There was a disagreement," Sandover muttered. "I do not wish to indulge the hostility of superstitious peasants." He started up the ladder to the hayloft, pausing halfway. "And I am not to be disturbed. Is that clear?"

"I'll try, but you're always a little disturbed," Patrice said, stroking the bristly brush over the horse's rump in smooth circles.

"You know what I mean."

"*Bon nuit.*"

The boys soon opened a cask of grog, and by midnight were roaring drunk. It might have been done out of spite of Sandover, but Cary expected they'd be no different any other night. He and Jaime stayed aloof, having found a corner where several hay bales were stacked together, providing a dry if prickly bench.

As the crew broke out in a stomping, clapping chorus a shriek rose from the hayloft. Sandover appeared at the edge, straw sticking out of his hair, violence in his wheeling eyes. He scrambled down the ladder like a silky pink rat and broke through the circle of drunken men.

"*Assez!*" he cried, stomping his foot. A ripple of subtle force swept outwards, knocking the men off their perches and making the fire flare. Sparks landed on a nearby clump of straw and dung, which caught alight.

"For God's sake," Jamie hissed. He jumped down from the shelf of hay. Sandover was dancing about, flapping his arms and doing nothing to stop the fire as it jumped to another bit of straw. "*Sacre cœur*, Patrice, put that down," Gordo said as Patrice made to heave the barrel of liquor at the flames. "I told you, fire loves the liquor."

"Stand back," Jaime said sharply. His feet planted, he stared at the flames, reached out his hand, then made a downward motion like striking a drum. The flames flattened and died, leaving a thin trail of wet-smelling smoke.

"Bravo, Mr. Skye," Sandover crowed as the rest began to mutter amongst themselves. "I am pleased to see you take command of your abilities." He made to shake hands with Jaime, who jerked away from him with a look of disgust.

"Just know that if I wanted to, I could have let you burn."

ALONE

The next day they met the flies. Met, fought, and were resolutely defeated by, despite the salve, which smelled of pine needles and cat urine and kept the enormous flies from biting but not from buzzing around one's eyes and mouth and lighting on one's collar. While they rested at midday, he watched Cary fashion a fringe for his hat, tying bits of bark to long blades of grass then threading the grass through holes he had punched in the brim with his knife. It gave him the look of a beaded lamp-shade, but he seemed to be spitting out fewer flies.

"You doing alright?" Cary asked when they were moving again, speaking low under the creak of the wagon and incessant cursing of the boys.

"I'm fine."

"I worried you might have had a rough night, is all."

"I don't need you coddling me." That it was true only cut harder, for when Jaime had at last fallen asleep it had been to dream of the tunnel, the flood. He had awoken panting and drenched to the skin. Every step northward took them closer to danger. A danger he could not see, as though he still groped through that subterranean canal, waiting for an unimaginable death to swallow him whole.

"It's not coddling to want to help you," Cary grumbled.

"You're not meant to help me. You're meant to keep me from running away."

"Where would you go?"

"Compared to this death march? I'd take my chances."

"Go on then," Cary said, his hard face unchanged, so that Jaime had no sense if he was at all serious. "If you're so sure of yourself."

"Come with me."

He grunted, lowering his grim brow. "I can't."

"Then help me destroy him."

"Don't try."

"Would you stop me?"

"If I had to."

"You'll protect me from his violence, make sure I'm fed, show me every kindness but this."

"It's not mere kindness you're asking of me."

The convoy jolted to a halt as the wheel struck another deep furrow, for the mud from yesterday's rain still lay thick on the road. While the others heaved and ho'd, trying to roll the wagon out of the rut, Jaime quietly tested his newest skill. Early this morning, he'd pulled the water from a fresh green leaf, watching it shrink then curl then crumble to powder in his hand. He brought the same focus of mind to the muck beneath the wagon's wheels, willing the moisture to boil itself into vapour and dissipate.

"By God, boys, that's got it!" Patrice cried as the wagon jerked forward out of the drying crevice. "Can't wait to get off these dirty old roads and onto the water."

"The what?" Sandover had been standing on the roadside, swatting away the flies with his closed fan, and now grabbed Patrice's sleeve. "What do you mean, water?"

"There's only so much road to go on when you're hauling this much whatnot. Didn't Gordo show you the maps?"

"He told me we were going overland!"

"What do you think we're doing right now, Mr. Silky Pants?"

Trembling with rage, Sandover let go of the man's arm and raised his clawed hand, ready to strike. Paused, then clenched his hand into a fist, his eyes pinching closed as he muttered under his breath.

"What's that now?"

"None of your damned business."

"What hold does he have over you?" Jaime asked Cary as a fuming Sandover stomped ahead up the road.

"It's not him," he replied, shoulders moving like two boulders trying to climb over each other. "It's the man he serves. All of this is on his orders."

"Whose orders?"

"The duke's."

"Which duke?"

"Dunno. Didn't much feel like asking at the time. Was doing my best not to cack my drawers in fright."

"Someone frightened *you*?"

His voice dropped to a subterranean drone, his words cold as stone. "There's something unholy about that man. And I've met some wicked men. Sandover's as much his slave as we are."

"What does he want?"

"Power, like all men who already have too much. I don't know how this venture serves his cause, but you can bet that's what he's after. More power."

"We can't let them control us."

"I have no choice. But I'll do all I can to protect you."

"If Sandover wants me dead you won't be able to stop him."

"He doesn't want you dead. You're too useful."

"Please, Cary. Tell me what he wants from me."

"If you knew, would it make a difference?"

Yes, and no. Yes, because he wished to be forewarned. No, because he was bound to this adventure, whether he wished to be or not, and knowing what awaited wouldn't diminish its danger. Yes, because he wanted some sign that Cary's friendship wasn't lost to him. No, because then he'd know with certainty that they were none of them free.

The grey sky hid the sun and the green trees hid all the rest of the world so that the hours melted into a single endless plod from nowhere to nowhere. They were starting up yet another hill when Gordo cried out, grabbing the horse's halter to stop the wagon. He down the long curve of the valley along the path a householder had cleared through the thick forest. "By God, boys, did you see that?"

"*Qu'est-ce que c'est?* Show me, buddy," Patrice said, squinting along Gordo's quivering arm.

"There in them bushes at the bend."

Stroking his beard, Patrice gasped. "Could it be a saskahach?"

"Is that some kind of animal?" Jaime asked.

"He means sasquatch," Gordo said as Patrice went to whisper in Cesar's ear. "Big hairy man thing, lives in woods just like this. We seen one last year. A right hairy bastard he was too. I'll be damned if I didn't just see one off there in them bushes."

"If such a thing happened to exist," Sandover droned, "you couldn't possibly see it at this distance with those lantern-glass eyes."

"You don't know what them eyes have seen," Patrice said.

"Not a damned thing, I expect."

"That's where you might be wrong there, Mr. Fancy Coat and Shoes," Gordo said, plucking at the shoulder of Sandover's satin coat. "There's things in these woods you don't want to be looking at with your regular people eyes."

He smacked Gordo's hand away. 'I know where I'd start," he gritted.

"What's that you say?"

"I said can we keep on?"

The going was slow on the rough road and they reached the town of Holland Landing late in the evening. From here they would travel up the canal to Lake Simcoe. Though the boys had planned to continue by boat to Georgian Bay, Sandover had asked, then insisted forcibly, that they journey overland from a town on the northwest shore, taking what appeared on the map to be a much shorter route, a distance of less than twenty miles across lightly settled country.

They pitched tents with several other groups of travelers on a grassy pitch not far from the small dockyard. Sandover had done his disappearing act while the others were still setting up camp. If Jaime ever saw Voight again, that non-man in human form who worked for Adrian, he would ask if Sandover was anything like him, able to step out of the world and into another. He doubted it, for Sandover was too humanly robust, whereas Voight was, well, was not. Was a faceless void in a suit of clothes who could wink in and out of existence at will, and who assisted Adrian at the behest of his own unspoken interests.

Thoughts of his friend—not of Voight but of Adrian, sensible, sensitive, generous Adrian—churned in Jaime's hollow heart. Did he know about Jaime's abduction? Was he even now leading a magical army in pursuit, or was this duke powerful enough to interfere in the laws of their world? Jaime's world, like it or not, for he was bound up in this wretched business as long as he remained in Sandover's control.

Being an active trading port, the little town was lively, with several public houses spread between the two main intersections of the northbound road. Seated with the crew at a pair of tables in the side room of a busy tavern, Jaime accepted a bowl of fish and corn soup from the shared tureen. Gordo was seated across from him, his jaw working rapidly. His eyes swiveling, he drew an inch long fishbone from between his lips.

"Don't want to be swallowing that," he said, flicking the bone onto the muddy floor where a passing foot immediately trod it into the muck.

"Did you really see a creature in the woods today?" Jaime asked as Gordo went back to scraping his bowl clean.

"I seen something. And believe you me, there's plenty out there to see."

"Monsters?"

"The sasquatch, he's no monster. Least I don't think of him as such. Sometimes if you're out in the woods by yourself too much, you forget how to be around people, but I know there's a man under all that hair of his."

"What if it was a bear you saw?"

"What if it was? There's stinking big bears all around, and wolves and coyotes and you name it. So don't be wandering off, Mr. Town and City. You don't need to sneak off into them woods to hide what you and your big friend do."

"I don't know what you mean."

Gordo blew out a breath through his lips. "As long as you know, your secret's safe with us," he muttered, his eyebrows crawling over his brow.

"What secret are you talking about?"

"You and the big fella."

"I don't understand."

Gordo exhaled again, his eyes wheeling. "You and him are sharing a tent tonight, aren't yas? So? Why's that?"

"Because that's all there was and there's no room for a third person and...oh. You think we're lovers."

Gordo's big eyes swelled even more. "*Sacrebleu...*" he muttered through his teeth. "If you're just gonna come out and say it—"

"We're not, though."

"You don't need to lie."

"I'm not lying. He's nothing to me."

"If you say so."

"You know what he is to me? My jailor."

Needing to get away from this reeking tavern, these baseless beliefs, Jaime pushed aside his uneaten soup and stood up. The man sitting behind him stirred then got to his feet as well. Cary, whose face showed no sign of having heard, though he couldn't have missed a word. He followed Jaime outside.

"Must you be at me night and day?" Jaime jammed his clammy hands in his pockets to keep from gathering any more dew as they walked.

"It's my job" he replied. "And are we not on the same side anymore?"

"There are no sides. We're all victims of that cursed duke of yours."

"Then why are we at odds?"

"You tell me."

"You think I've been telling people we're sodomites?"

"Someone has been."

"People see what they want to see."

"Maybe if you weren't stuck to me like a bad smell they'd have nothing to see."

The boys had provided themselves a pair of army tents, broad, sturdy structures with a high ridge pole so one might stand up inside. The third tent was that in miniature, so low Cary had to crawl to get in. Inside was dark as a tomb, Cary's great bulk taking up most of the bedroll as he sat down to take off his boots.

"They haven't made this easy," he grunted.

"You'll be sleeping half on top of me."

"Better get used to it, there'll be a lot of nights like this."

"Don't say that so loudly or they really will think we're lovers."

"Doesn't matter," Cary muttered. "I'd not have you for love or money."

"Like I'd let you lay a finger on me, you benighted lump of clay."

Though the night was cool, the tent held their warmth and the air was soon stifling. The other man was a bristling irritation: his droning breath, his peculiar sharp scent, his presence a reminder that Jaime would always be alone.

PORTAGE

Jaime spent most of the night prodding Cary in the back with his elbows and grumbling to himself about lumps of clay and false pretences and other things that couldn't be helped. When it was barely light he left the tent, and though by rights Cary should have followed him, he lay for several minutes more, weighed down by misery. This northern country didn't speak his language, the stony black hills mute beneath his feet, the blanketing forests dark and desolate-feeling. And they had barely begun, had miles to go and then... He doubted even Sandover understood what they were meant to be doing, for the duke was cracked if he trusted his sneering minion with the whole of the truth.

This early in the day, most boats launching belonged to fishermen and the dockyard was quiet. A special sort of quiet, not the blunt, wind-swept silence of the desert but a muted softness: the dip of oars in smooth water, the rustle of leaves, the warbling song of a solitary bird, its black wings banded with red, which clung to the stem of a reed.

Jaime was sitting at the end of the jetty, his feet dangling. Cary nearly left him alone, but unlike the vastness of the ocean, Jaime could cross the mile wide river in a matter of minutes, or travel along it until he reached the next settlement, never to be seen again. He waited for Cary to sit beside him then got up and started back towards land. "Don't be like this," Cary said.

Jaime stopped. "What does it matter to you?" he said in a harsh, unhappy tone.

"We have to put up with each other for a while longer. Can you not make it harder than it has to be?"

"You know my feelings. If you won't help me then don't consider yourself my friend."

"You don't understand."

He came a few paces nearer, his bitter expression softening. "Then help me understand. I don't care what you've had to do to stay alive. I've done dreadful things, God knows. You made me think I could count on you. Now I have to ask myself if that was a lie—"

"I meant what I said. Together, we've got the better of him."

"Then why won't you fight? What are you afraid of?"

"It's not him that frightens me. It's not him who's bound me to this."

"Ah, yes, your friend the duke," Jaime said, his eyes hardening. "Should you ever happen to see his grace again, you can tell him from me to get royally fucked." He walked away, leaving Cary at the end of the dock, alone with his misery.

They surrendered the hired cart and took passage on a small paddle barge for the next leg of the journey, up the Holland River and along the western shore of Lake Simcoe. Sandover fidgeted like an opium eater from the minute he stepped aboard the clanking, stinking vessel, as if the serpent-beast Eckhart had described was stalking them through the glassy brown water and not in a different lake several hundred miles away.

Driven by tireless steam, their ship reached Kempenfelt Bay and the town of Barrie that afternoon. Like many of the settlements in the area, the town had served as a garrison in the American war, due to its position at the end of the portage to Lake Huron.

"What do you mean, there's no road?" Sandover said as they waited ashore for the cargo to be offloaded.

"That's what *portage* means, Mr. Sandwicher," Gordo said as they watched the bargemen wrestle the heavier of the crates onto a canvas sling to hoist it onto the jetty. "If there's no road and no river, you gotta port it yourself through whatever's in the way. I'm right sure that we said so."

"Impossible," Sandover breathed, groping for his hat to fan himself. "His grace is out of his mind. The duke can't expect me to see this through."

"Is one of you English a duke?" asked Patrice.

"No, and be glad of it," Sandover hissed, shoving his hat on his head. "And for the last time, not one of us is English!"

It took two days to travel the twenty miles. Two long, grinding, dull and sweaty days of manhandling three long canoes and Sandover's bloody boxes along an army trail climbing through unending forest. The flies had dispersed, to be replaced by mosquitoes, who were undeterred by the fringe of bark plugs hanging from Cary's hat.

Jaime was unbothered. The same power that had kept the flies from biting him prevented the much lighter mosquitoes from even landing. That left him surrounded at all times by a cloud of the wretches, who would light savagely on whomever else came close. As a consequence he spent much of his time alone, trailing the others, Cary looking back again and again to be sure he still followed.

By the time they reached the head of the river Sandover was almost eager to board a canoe. His glossy yellow hair drew the mosquitos like flies to honey. Unlike Jaime, his magic had no power over the insects, and his neck and hands were pocked with their red bites. A dozen or more swarmed about his head as Patrice held the canoe steady for him to board.

"It's easy going now, Lord Songbirder," he said cheerfully.

"How much further must we travel?" Sandover said as he gingerly lowered himself onto the slatted seat amidships.

"'Bout fifteen miles to Wasaga."

"Excellent."

"Then over to the Big Island."

"Oh yes. The island."

"Then it's just another five, ten, well maybe like forty miles, to the place you want us to take you to."

"*Merde...*" Sandover flinched, slapping his cheek, then pulled his hand away to glare at the murdered insect.

"What's all the way out there you want to get to so bad?" Patrice asked, swinging one dripping leg over the side of the canoe while kicking off with the other to get the boat off the gravel.

"I cannot say," he replied icily, wiping off the blood on his stained handkerchief.

"Just seems like you don't want to be doing this."

"What is the purpose of your questions?"

"Just asking."

As the lightest person Jaime sat with the heaviest cargo, Sandover with the smaller box. After the drudgery of the trail the canoes fairly flew through the forest, borne on the downhill current towards the lake. They covered the fifteen miles by evening and stopped a night in the little town of Wasaga, where Cary endured a third night of Jaime's bristling ire for nothing more than the sin of existing too near him.

In the morning they boarded another steamer. Canoes and all, for they would be needed to travel to the site. Sandover had persuaded his way into the wheelhouse, and could be seen through the glass, surveying the lake through a long glass as if the water teemed with their quarry. Jaime did much the same, standing at the prow, his hands on the rail, gazing at the water as it crested around the hull. Cary lingered by the corner of the wheelhouse, wanting to keep an eye on him without overbearing.

"I know you're there," Jaime called. "You needn't worry."

"I can if I want."

He sagged, his head dropping. "I wish you wouldn't." Before Cary replied, he walked away, keeping his head down as he passed, leaving Cary feeling that much more alone.

The landing at Manitoulin was much as Cary expected for a minor trading post in a largely unsettled district, being a long wooden jetty with a few battered skiffs and pole barges moored for running cargo from bigger ships. Rather than use these, their cargo was boarded directly into the canoes, and the party paddled in to shore, where they pulled up onto a gravelly spit at the heart of the shallow bay.

"*Mon Dieu...*" Sandover murmured as he took in the sight. The dockyard consisted of the long jetty and a large timber-sided building. A hand-painted shield fixed to the wall declared it the property of the Hudson's Bay Company. A few other log houses stood about the dusty clearing. Another was under construction, men in their shirt-sleeves climbing on the bare rafters, the blows of their hammers ringing in the quiet.

As they hauled the canoes further up the spit, Little George, the spokesman for the Iroquois guides, came down from the trading house to meet them. The boys greeted him warmly, speaking to him in their raw French dialect, Gordo swapping a few phrases in the Iroquois' language.

Another man emerged from the building, wearing the local backcountry garb of buckskin trousers and woolen jacket, a wide brimmed leather hat shading his smooth face. Sandover glanced his way idly, then looked again. He hissed in an urgent breath, his eyes popping behind his swollen cheeks. Muttering in French, he began to fuss with his clothes, straightening his wilted stock.

"Who's that?" Gordo asked Cary, twisting his head to bring first one eye then the next to bear on the stranger. "Something a bit funny about him, you think?"

Cary could feel the power held within the unknown man. Looking made it worse, his pale face an expressionless mask with the rigid artificiality of a porcelain doll. His vague nub of a nose supported a pair of glasses with darkened lenses which concealed his eyes completely.

"Voight..." Jaime murmured, standing to Gordo's other side. "I knew a man without a face."

"How can you not have a face?"

"There was nothing there," he replied. "Just a void in the shape of a head. Void..." He laughed, a single bitter *ha*. "What a silly joke," he said. "His name was Voight Nihilo. Nothing-Nothing."

"This one don't look like a nothing," Gordo muttered.

"It's a mask," Cary said. "He's not of this world."

"*Sacre cœur*, fellas, what have you got us into?"

Little George's smile had fallen. "This sure is some interesting company you're keeping, boys," he said levelly. "You better hope it's worth what they're paying you to keep it."

THE DUKE'S MAN

For the past few days Jaime had done all he could to separate himself from Cary's friendship. He'd succeeded to the extent he had convinced himself that they were Sandover's captives, that there was no duke at all. That Cary would speak no more of it was proof there was nothing to speak of.

The arrival of the blank faced man had undone Jaime's resolve. Everything about him was deeply *wrong*, from the blank, bony face that never changed to the glinting glass of his dark glasses to his complete absence of smell. This unnerved Jaime more than anything, for his nose was ordinarily sensitive to a painful extreme. Even Adrian's peculiar friend and helpmate Voight had registered as a whiff of metallic stone and the scent of his clothes. The duke's man smelled of nothing at all. Sandover meanwhile was beside himself with servile enthusiasm, bowing and nodding and grinning like the French courtier he was any time the duke's man was about.

With the guides they made a significant armada, the boys' three large canoes shadowed by the Iroquois' smaller, swifter craft. At Little

George's suggestion, they embarked at once for the campsite several miles west along the southern coast of the island.

In mere minutes they had left behind the stink and clatter of the little port. The quiet was astonishing, the lake dominating the horizon in three directions. Even the heavily forested land to their right was absent the sounds—and smells—Jaime was accustomed to in Britain: the clang of distant church bells, the reek and ring of a village smithy, the scent of cut hay rolling across the fields. This land smelled of stone and sap and smoke, of frigid nights, and brilliant skies. Of water, cold and blind and deep, deeper than a lake had any right to be, his tuned awareness sensing such vastness that he shuddered.

They landed at the site near dusk. For the last two hours the setting sun had been in their eyes, and the forest seemed impossibly dark. Unsure of his place, exhausted from every aspect of the journey, he huddled on a rock near the water while the others went about building the tents, lighting a fire. Soon the smell of cooked meat and barley called him towards the ring of light and warmth.

The unspeaking Cesar was tending the cookpot hanging over the fire from a tall three-legged iron stand. Jaime accepted a tin plate of a heavy, pine-tasting porridge from him and refused a mug of grog from Patrice. Someone long ago had fashioned rude benches from fallen logs, the bark long gone and the wood satiny with age. Jaime took the last seat free, between Cary and Gordo, who now set his plate carefully on the uneven surface of the bench. He cleared his throat and the other boys fell silent.

"So, Lord Sand...over?" he started, cocking an eye at Sandover, who rolled his eyes and his wrist in acknowledgment, for they had yet to say his name correctly. "Do you mind telling us all what we're doing all the way out here?"

Sandover glanced at the duke's man, whose expressionless face looked even more deathly in the flaring up-light of the fire. "We are here on an expedition, my good man," he began in his most triumphant tone. "An heroic escapade."

"Heroic?" Cary snorted. "Pull the other leg, why don't you?"

"I mean it with great sincerity, Mr. Robb," Sandover oozed, in his element when lying. "We shall do what no one has done in a century, if ever before."

"Enough chatter, get to the point."

"Yes, tell them about the creature," Jaime said.

"Creature?" Patrice asked. "You mean like an animal?"

"A primitive life form," Sandover replied. "Brought here by our employer many years ago. It dwells in a cavern close to this locale."

"So what are we doing with it?"

"We are going to catch it."

"Impossible," Jaime said bluntly as the others began to mutter together. "Who could catch a serpent that size?"

"Serpent?" Gordo blurted, his head whipping round. "You didn't say nothing about no dirty snakes."

"It's not a snake."

"Then what is it?"

"It is not a creature that you know." All fell silent and turned toward the duke's man, for though his lips had not moved, no one doubted that he had spoken, his words passing tonelessly into Jaime's mind without touching his ears. "It is a creature from Deep Time," the man went on, his head pivoting slowly to show his uncanny face to each of them. "A relic of the ancients."

"His Grace intended to retrieve it somewhat earlier, I believe," Sandover said with false brightness. "To his misfortune, certain, how shall I say, historical events interrupted."

"Like what?"

"Napoleon, for one," he replied, his smile twisting unpleasantly. "Otherwise we might have come to fetch it some several decades ago."

"Can we get back to the underwater snake business," Gordo said tightly.

"You needn't worry," Sandover said, merry once more. "We've a man who's suited for the task. Aren't you Mr. Skye?"

His heart thrummed with terror as all eyes turned on him. "I know nothing of this creature," he stammered.

"Perhaps not," Sandover said sweetly, "But you will find it regardless. It must be you, Mr. Skye. You who can go where none of us are able."

"I'll die down there!"

"You cannot drown—"

"Yes, but I can freeze. Or be eaten, or...you're out of your mind if you think I can help you."

"You have no choice."

He ought to stop fighting, stay silent and safe, not raise Sandover's ire any further, but he'd never felt such a burning need to prove he was not beaten. "You love this, don't you?" he said, "watching people suffer?"

"You will mind your tongue," Sandover retorted, his nostrils quivering.

"Or what, you'll throw me in the lake? All your magic, and his," he spat, gesturing at the false-faced man. "*And* your cursed duke's, and *I'm* your plan? I'm to tame a monster? Me? If you think I'm capable of such a thing then you truly are mad, madder than I've ever been accused of being. And you," and he turned to the duke's man, his dark glasses reflecting the leaping flames. "I hope what you hear is heard by your foul master, because he should know I wish him to rot in hell."

He turned his back and left the warmth of the fire, not caring if Sandover struck him down. A swift death was preferable to this lunacy. Relying on sound and smell to guide him away from the water, he made his way cautiously to their miserable little tent, crawled inside and shivered until he slept.

He woke to the sound of birdsong and the quiet rumble of Cary's breath. The canvas showed grey and not black, so he crawled out of the cocoon of blankets, retrieved his sorry, sodden boots, and left the tent.

Mist lay about the camp, glowing gold in the first rays of sun, the sound of the water a muted ripple against the bluntly shelving shore. Alone, unseen, Jaime held out his hand and waited for the droplets to form on his palm. Britain had its springs and streams, its landlocked tarns on Yorkshire hillsides, but he had never felt anything like this, the salt-less alkalinity of water so far from the sea. Dashing the prickling drops from his hand, he carried on towards the trees, where the mist lay thinner.

On the left side of the little bay, a spit of gravel ran down into the water. The fire-pit was a few yards from this, beyond it a wide pitch of open sandy ground where the tents stood. Behind these rose the forest, silvery aspen and maples with their darker, broader leaves shoulder to shoulder with wind-warped pines and cedar.

An old tree had fallen in a recent storm, leaving a bright clearing. Someone in plain clothing was seated on the fallen trunk, their back to the camp, and Jaime was about to call out when he sensed the man's uncanny stillness. A fearful sweat broke across his shoulderblades as slowly, scarcely moving his body, the duke's man turned his head to gaze at Jaime.

In his hand was a bird, mute and docile, its dove-pink head unmoving. The duke's man held up the bird, regarding it with soulless indifference. For a moment Jaime thought he would crush the poor thing, but he opened his hand flat. After a little the bird stirred, then sprang into flight.

How he envied that bird. The duke's man was getting to his feet and without an ounce of shame Jaime turned and ran, back to the camp where the evil was easier to comprehend. He slowed as he passed the tents, approaching the shore with care. The big canoes had been laid upside down on the roughly cut logs to keep rain from gathering in them, but the smaller bark-hulled canoes of the Iroquois were not among them. Heart sinking, he made a circuit of the campground and discovered that their tipis were gone as well.

He debated rousing the others, but they'd know soon enough. Gordo found him by the fire, prodding the smoldering coals with a stick.

"Where's Little George and them?" he asked, drawing up a short log to sit beside Jaime.

"Packed up and gone home."

"*Sacre bleu...*" Gordo sprang to his feet, staring about as horror dawned on his sunburnt face. "Then what are we still doing here? I don't want nothing to do with none of Mr. Fancy's lake snakes!"

"You might not have a choice. He's more dangerous than any animal. Please don't underestimate him."

"We'll see who's under whose estimating."

"I mean it. He'll kill you and not think twice."

Gordo sat again, his eyes wheeling. "Would he really?"

"I don't have time to list all the cruel things he's done. To me, to others. To anyone who crosses him."

"Why's he got to catch this thing so bad?"

Cary was crawling out of their tent, and Jaime nodded towards him. "Ask him. He knows more than I do."

"What happened between you and the big fella?" Gordo asked, shifting closer. "You aren't as friendly as you used to be."

"I can't afford to be friendly."

"It doesn't hurt though. Especially if we're stuck out here with Mr. So-and-So and his ghost. Sometimes friends is all you got."

Friends: Jaime had known so few in his three-odd decades. People he had met on the wards, for many of those confined were not there due to any mental ailment but because they were an inconvenience. Unmarried aunts, aging fathers, sweet-tempered mollies whose parents had relegated them to the asylum in hopes of scaring them back onto the straight and narrow. There one day and gone the next. Or Jaime was the one released, to discover his old friendships had withered. New ones were ever harder to commence, for who wished to be friends with a madman?

The only friend he'd ever loved, he'd left behind. Unless he counted Cary, who had shown his gruff devotion time and again, despite the danger to himself. Together, they were stronger. But were they strong enough?

LAST WORDS

Other than a few lumps of charcoal and some small holes in the ground, the Iroquois had disappeared from the campsite without leaving a trace. The loss of their local knowledge, hired hands, and more specifically their canoes had the boys in deep discussion of how to achieve Sandover's ambitions. As the ever-silent Cesar and Patrice led their pair of underlings into the forest to gather supplies, Gordo explained to Cary and Jaime how to build a raft.

By dint of his strength and blunt ignorance of all things water-borne, Cary was sent to help drag the dozen or so stout felled tree from the forest to the shore. Here they barked the logs, for the pine trunks were sappy and had picked up every bit of leaf and grime along the way. They trimmed away any protruding branches, then with the adze they planed one side of each log to a relatively level surface. Gordo led them in roping the trunks together, not on shore but in the knee deep water off the shingle.

Slowly the rough platform took shape, and by mid-afternoon he called a rest. Groaning, the others slogged up the shingle to dry land. Jaime remained in the water a little longer, walking around the raft, touching it here and there, as though he could test its seaworthiness with his hands.

"Cary…" He waded out of the water, his bare feet pink from the chill. "Can I speak to you?"

"You're speaking to me right now."

"I meant properly. I haven't been fair to you, I don't think."

"How so?"

"I've been telling myself you're part of the problem, but you've no more say in this than I do."

"Nor do any of us."

Even Sandover, attached to the duke's man like a whipped dog, bowing and grinning in his presence, ever on alert in his absence. Still nameless, rarely speaking, the eerie man haunted the campground like a wraith, silently appearing from behind a tree or tent when one didn't expect it, his black glasses like the polished eyes of an insect, unblinking and void of humanity.

"Anyway, that's what I wanted to say," Jaime went on. "I'm sorry that I've been so prickly towards you. Whatever debt you owe this duke—"

"There's no debt. I'm here to get back what's mine."

"So it's blackmail."

"I can't say more."

Jaime was about to reply but closed his mouth, his face hardening as he caught sight of something behind Cary.

"It's him, isn't it?" The duke's man, the wraith, his black eyes boring into the back of Cary's neck like twin needles.

"Do you think there are even eyes behind those—" Jaime broke off, gripping his forehead in anguish. "Lord help me, why did I let myself think that?"

Cary clasped Jaime's slim shoulder, bony from days of trail rations. "Don't let him in your mind. You've got bigger worries than some spook who never talks and doesn't do a thing."

"The not doing a thing is what worries me the most."

That evening Jaime was more withdrawn than usual, his head lowered whenever he wasn't watching Cary across the fire. He stirred when Cary did, however, and followed him to the tent, where he crawled into the envelope of blankets without griping about Cary's size or smell or intelligence.

Listening to Jaime's quiet breath, Cary thought back on his softened mood that afternoon, and his apology. Losing Jaime's trust had hurt him more than he'd let himself feel, and he'd spent the last several days telling himself that the loss was tolerable. A fair price to pay in exchange for his kinfolk's dreamings. He'd put his faith in a man—a devil, that duke—who'd done nothing but hurt him, and wounded a man who'd shown him nothing but care.

"Jaime..." he murmured.

"Hmm..."

"I'm sorry."

"For what?"

"For turning so cold on you. For being no better. You're...you're my last friend on Earth. I don't want to muck that up."

"Me neither."

In the dark he felt rather than saw Jaime roll towards him. Pressed against Cary's shoulder, he spoke in a breathy whisper close to his ear. "You understand this is our last chance to get free. We'll never have another."

"Where would we go?" he mumbled in reply, barely moving his lips.

"Anywhere. We've that tinderbox of Strike's so we won't want for light or warmth. I can smell cook-fires for miles. We'll find a band of natives or some trading company men and beg for help. Someone will listen."

He was strongly tempted to agree. He longed to stop living this way, being held hostage by Sandover, a man he wouldn't piss on to save his life if he caught fire. What if the duke had lied? What if there was no link, and the stolen barks in the duke's treasure house weren't his kin's embodied dreamings but a mere glimpse of their truth, as a Catholic's bible was to the received word of God. Was he brave enough to find out the hard way, by breaking his oath to that foul man, betraying his orders, and heading into the unknown?

All was unknown, all was peril. He'd gotten used to not being afraid. To feeling invulnerable, protected by his strength, his hardness. To never wondering if what he did was right or wrong. All of that was gone, replaced by this bitter bemusement, a sense that he was buggered to hell no matter what he did.

"Jaime," he whispered.

"Hmm..."

"What he wants is impossible, right?"

"Of course."

"So maybe if you just went down once and had a look, found out for certain—"

Jaime stiffened, his breath hitching. "What if I refuse? Will you force it on me?"

"It's not for my sake."

"Then who's? Please tell me."

Still Cary hesitated, but what did he gain from keeping this secret? Why divide himself from Jaime now, when the man had reached past his fears and offered the olive branch? "A couple years back, I found work as a guide. I was trying to get free of my rotten life, so I went outback, back to my country, where I'd been born. Some white men offered me what seemed like a fortune to take them round some special places. Sacred places where I knew I shouldn't take them, but I was tired of starving. They stole from my kin, and when I came after them, they did the same to me as I did to you. I woke up on a ship bound for England."

"These men worked for the duke?"

"They did."

"What did they steal?"

"Our dreams."

"Can such a thing be stolen?"

"There are ways. The Deathless Duke is like no other man. Knows things no one should know. How to strip a man's soul from his body, how to tear apart time, end the world. Condemn him and all his ancestors to wander through the dreamless dark, no songs to guide them, no light to find." To say more was to bring the terror nearer. Jaime was silent for so long Cary was sure he had fallen asleep, until he rolled towards Cary again.

"I'll go down. I don't know what I'll find but..."

"I won't let him hurt you."

"I know."

The next morning they towed the raft off the shingle and out into the lake. Cary felt the moment when they passed beyond the shelf of rock that held up the island and entered deep water, as the solidity gave way to the unknown. Looking back, the land seemed very far away, the raft pitifully small.

It dipped alarmingly under his weight as he clambered from the canoe. He crawled to the centre where he crouched, unable to rise to his feet, unable to raise his head, for there was nothing to see but water. No land, no safety, no hope. He'd spent his strength dragging these logs to the shore, yet the raft was as a leaf in a hurricane against the enormity of the lake. Jaime crouched before him.

"You can't swim, can you?" he asked in the hushed murmur he used when Sandover was near. Cary shook his head, speech beyond him, this sense of heart-crushing dread surpassing the dislocation he had felt crossing the ocean. Closing his eyes, Jaime laid his hand over Cary's. A soft warmth began to spread up Cary's arm, anchoring him to Jaime, to the firm cradle of the trees who had given their lives to bear theirs up. Deeper, through the water to the stone floor of the lake and into the heart of the earth.

Jaime opened his eyes. "Did that work?"

"Suppose so. Don't feel so much like I'm going to upchuck over the side."

"I won't let anything happen to you. I promise."

He left Cary to absorb the warmth, let it filter through him, calm his fears. They would survive this reckless venture, together. They were stronger together.

DESCENT

They lashed one of the canoes to the side of the raft to serve as a store. The second drifted in the current at the end of a short mooring line. Coyne and Tench took the third and returned to the island, for there was only room for so many people on the gently listing raft.

"Well, Mr. Skye, are you game for a little fishing?" Sandover oozed.

"Go to hell."

His preening smirk fell away. "*Pardon*?"

"You heard me. You can shove your jolly act up your rear end. You know not a one of us wants to be here. Not even you." Jaime began to undress.

Sandover frowned, looking him up and down. "What are you doing?"

"Have you thought of bringing anything for me to wear after I huck myself in the lake for you and your rotten duke?" Jaime asked, shrugging out of his braces. "If not, I'd better keep my clothes dry, hadn't I?"

He kept his shirt on mainly to deprive Sandover the sight of his nudity. Feeling very pale, he crouched at edge of the raft and peered into the water. There was no judging the depth, the water clear but darkly so, despite the glitter of sun across its surface.

"This is useless. I won't be able to see a thing down there."

"Of that you have no fear," Sandover said. From the trunk he retrieved a glass sphere somewhat larger than his hand. Another smaller sphere floated within it, filled with a swirling grey mist. Sandover passed his hand over it and murky mist brightened until it glowed like a lamp.

With the sphere secured in sort of net that he could sling around his chest, Jaime sat on the edge of the raft again and dipped his feet in the water. Cold blazed up his shins, searing his bare skin.

"Faith!" He sprang to his feet and backed away from the edge. "The water's like ice."

"It's midsummer," Sandover gritted.

"If you're so eager, why don't you go for a dip yourself?"

"You will obey me, Skye. Or you will suffer."

"How can I suffer more than I have already?"

"Shall we discover?" Grinning foully at Jaime, he flung his lacy hand towards Cary, still crouching amid ships. Groaning, Cary slumped forward, clutching his chest.

"Leave him alone!"

"No." He closed his fist. Cary screamed breathlessly, his face purpling, his eyes wild. Sandover twisted his hand and Cary's body jerked sideways, towards the edge of the raft.

"Damn you!" Jaime cried as Sandover let Cary drop gasping to the timber. "You and you're your wretched master, and that demon on the shore, everything you are."

"Watch your tongue, Mr. Skye," Sandover spat, his eyes veiled, his teeth bared.

"Shove your *Mr. Skye*, you monster. I'm not yours to command."

"Is that what you think?" He shut his hand as if grabbing a man by the shirt then made a gesture like casting something away. A wave of force swept over them, jerking Jaime's breath from his mouth and sweeping Cary off the raft and into the water. He at once began sinking, grabbing at the water, his feet barely stirring.

"Leave him," Sandover snarled as Patrice made to leap off the raft.

"But—ahh!" Grabbing his head, Patrice dropped to his knees.

"Do not tempt me."

"Bring him back!" Jaime shouted, barely stopping short of grabbing Sandover by the neck. Every second took Cary closer to death, his movements already growing feeble, his face full of terror. "He's going to drown."

"Do you think so?" Sandover drawled.

"Not if I can help it."

He closed his eyes, reaching his senses down into the darkness: *send him back. Send him back to me, don't take him from me, not now, not when he's all that I have...*

He thought of fountains and currents, of waterfalls running backwards, of waves bringing sailors home. He thought of the pond in the park, the great spouts of water leaping towards the sky. Picturing this, he reached out his hands and threw them skyward. Water leapt from the lake and fell back in two sparkling arcs.

Not enough to buoy up Cary's solid weight. He would make it enough. As Cary's anguished face slipped under the surface Jaime summoned every ounce of belief in himself and his powers, all the rage at the years he had lost and his want for the years still to live, and hurled his will towards the water: *rise and bring him back to me!*

He threw his up hands. The others shouted in mingled terror and awe as the raft tilted. A great geyser of water burst from the lake, bearing aloft a sputtering, flailing Cary and flinging him towards the raft with force.

"Bugger your lordship," Gordo grunted as Jaime leaped to grab Cary's arm. Grabbing a rope, he came to Jaime's aid and between them they helped Cary from the water.

"Hey, Mr. Skye," Patrice said as Cary lay gasping, water streaming from his hair and clothes. "Should we do something about this?"

"Of course you should, you cretin," Sandover shrieked, his voice oddly garbled. Jaime looked about, not seeing the mage until Patrice pointed towards the other side of the raft. Sandover was treading water, his embroidered silk coat splayed about him, his feet kicking frantically.

"It's all one to me," Patrice said. "To be honest, he's a bit of an arsehole."

As they gazed down at him Sandover made a sally, his shoulders rising clear of the water before he sank down again, gurgling. So tempting. Not to kill him but to simply not save him. Yet now that he was faced with the opportunity, Jaime knew that to do so was to cause himself the same spiritual harm that had so corrupted Lord Sandover. God help him, he didn't have it in him to let a man drown. Cruelty paid by cruelty was not justice.

"Arsehole he may be, but fish him out anyway."

It took three of them to drag Sandover and his weighty clothes aboard the raft. He sat in the canoe streaming water but making no complaint as they returned to the island, where he disappeared into his tent. Cary stayed by the fire, wrapped in blankets, his clothes propped on sticks to dry. Jaime stayed with him, though they didn't speak. What was there to be said? Their course was set, their choices narrowed down to this singular path: to do Sandover's bidding until they or he died.

Turning Cary's boots over to let the fire dry the insides, Jaime wondered if this was how one felt in wartime: huddling round a fire some foreign land, waiting to be hurled into battle by decree from a distant commander. He regretted the thought as the mage flung open his tent flap and came flouncing across the campground, his pink silk suit gleaming like a freshly cut rose, his golden hair curling softly across his shoulders. Rotten to the core.

"We have many hours of daylight, Mr. Skye. We will make another attempt."

"Damn you."

Sandover growled, a low rasp in the back of his throat. "Do not provoke me, Mr. Skye. Your dear friend has done all I needed of him, and kept you from rashly attempting to flee. I am happy to discover he is able to serve me in another way."

"I'm done serving you," Cary grated, gazing into the fire.

"You may think so, but I do not need your obedience." Sandover clenched his hand and thrust it forward. With a strangled grunt Cary lunged towards the fire as if to throw himself on it, the blanket falling from his bare shoulders to the dirt.

"Let him go!"

"Jaime!" he wheezed, his whole body shaking as he fought against the force dragging him forwards.

"Well, Mr. Skye?" Sandover said, his face as blank of feeling as the duke's demonic man.

"Damn your eyes, I'll do it. And may God have mercy on us."

Sandover released Cary, who slumped back on his heels, panting. As he mage sauntered away Jaime threw the blanket around his friend's trembling shoulders.

"What are you doing?" he asked as Cary heaved himself to his feet.

"Coming with."

"What if you end up in the water again?"

"Then tie me to the bloody raft. I'm not leaving you alone with him."

He would hear of nothing but, so Jaime drew most of the water from his clothing, a working which left his hands tingling. Chewing pemmican against the gnawing ache of hunger, he boarded the long canoe once more, sitting between Cary and Sandover as if he could shield his friend from the mage's cruelty.

This time they thought to bring blankets for after, but Jaime still undressed, not wanting to be encumbered by wet clothes. Sandover relit his gassy sphere and Jaime hung it across his chest where it burned without heat and did nothing to lift his fear.

He could not drown, but he could die. Shivering in the breeze whipping across the lake, he crouched at the edge of the raft once more. Every minute he waited was another minute of dread to endure, and so with the heaviest of hearts, he slipped from the raft and into the water.

Cold...cold as the night sky in the grip of midwinter. Worse and worse the deeper he went, for he was wholly exposed, the water pressing in on him from all sides. His lungs heavy, his life dependent on a miracle, he let himself sink another dozen feet. His limbs dragged through the gelid water, so unlike the frothy buoyancy of the sea, the cold sapping his energy. Sandover's glowing orb was a tiny spark, its pretty light of little help. If anything it made him an attraction to whatever lived here. With a shudder that had nothing to do with the cold, he wondered if that was part of the plan.

The raft was anchored atop a platform of rock that stood alone in much deeper water. Everywhere were similar columns and shelves lurking in the greenish gloom, carved from the edge of the island by wind and wave then whittled to nothing.

He swam along the edge of the platform, wary of going deeper. As he swam across a gap between two tumbled stacks he shuddered again. The water had a different taste, like city effluent polluting a stream. He had a sudden and very strong wish to surface. His skin prickling, he rolled and struck out for the raft, angling towards the surface as he went. Crossing back over the gap between the rocks, he caught the rotten taste again. A shadow moved in the depths, a monstrous form swelling at the base of the crevice. With the instinct of a man used to terror, Jaime began to swim much faster.

COLD COMFORT

Moments became minutes became an impossible passage of time without a sign of Jaime Skye. He hadn't sunk, rather had struck out swimming boldly downwards, shedding bubbles, Sandover's enchanted light around his neck making his pale limbs glow beneath the water, until even that had faded from view. Still they waited, as thin clouds stole across the sky, stealing the heat from the sun and darkening the water.

Gordo hunkered beside Cary where he sat at the centre of the raft. "We should have tied a rope to him too, eh, big fella?" he said in his kindly way.

"Bit late for that, I reckon."

"Wonder if Mr. Fancy has another of them lamps of his. We could hang it below so's he knows where we are."

"Him and whatever else is down there."

"Now don't you go thinking like that," Gordo said, poking him in the shoulder. "There's some dirty big fish in these waters but you don't think there's really a monster like the ghostman said, do ya? Do ya?"

"Dunno. I saw some drawings in Toronto. This pair of engineers had a piece of something. Some huge creature, but badly beat up."

"So he wasn't telling tales?" Gordo breathed, his drifting eyes converging on Cary for one uncanny moment.

"Dunno."

"Hey!" Patrice called. "Cesar's seen something." He pointed at a fluttering wake forming two hundred feet away, on the side opposite to the island. The thickening clouds had turned the water a slatey grey, the glinting, shimmering surface concealing everything below. And then it crested…

Gordo swore in his New World French, his eyes wheeling. Even Sandover shrieked in fear as a long reddish tentacle arched free of the water. At its end a cluster of writhing pink fronds surrounded a snapping beak like the mouth of an octopus. Ten feet long or more, the arm whipped about then slammed down on the surface of the lake, sending water spraying in all directions.

Or were there two now, or were they limbs of the same beast, as another fleshy length streaked through the air, raising a huge plume of water as it struck, perhaps its way of hunting. One wheeling arm swept low across the water and struck the side of the raft. As another arm came streaking from the other side, Sandover spat a slithering word and cast a violent pulse of destructive energy towards it. The fleshy appendage burst apart in a rancid spatter, green gobbets of its curious blood raining down on the water and raft. In a blink the other arms withdrew, leaving a pink and white object bobbing on the surface. Jaime, his skin flayed by the cold, his movements feeble.

"Rope!" Cary shouted, forcing himself to his feet. Gordo was at his side in a flash with a hank of rope. He tied the one end around Cary's waist, above the rope that tied him to the raft.

"Don' you worry, we're gonna get him back for ya."

"Just hurry!"

With Cesar behind to brace him, Gordo flung the other end of the line to Jaime. It fell short in the choppy water, but Gordo retrieved the rope and threw it again. "Got him! Heave, boys!"

Cary dug in his heels. As the rope slackened he drew it in hand over hand. And then Jaime was being pulled from the water and wrapped in a blanket, and Patrice lifted him and brought him to Cary.

He sank to his knees, Jaime's frail body unmoving in his arms. Suddenly Jaime lurched, twisting away from Cary as he vomited. Only water, but he had to have swallowed a ton of it, his body wracked by spasms again and again. His skin was slick with fear, his flesh cold to the touch, his limbs twitching like a man being beaten.

"What's wrong with him?" Cary asked.

"He's cold," Gordo said, crouching beside him.

"That can't be all."

"And half drowned and I don't know what. I never seen anything like what I seen today."

When Jaime seemed done bringing up water, Cary tucked a blanket around him then sat down to cradle him in his lap. The slender bloke still shivered, his face so pale it was nearly blue. The monstrous tendrils had subsided beneath the water, but Cary wouldn't feel safe until he had rock under him.

Gordo tensed, jutting out his chin, and Cary looked up to find Sandover standing over him

"*Aux innocents les mains pleines*," he drawled, a vile twist to his fleshy lips. "I do hope your *petit ami* is more useful tomorrow."

"Tomorrow? You're out of your bloody mind."

"You will do as I say, Mr. Robb."

"I might, but what can he do? Poor bugger's half dead. How's he going to be any use to you?"

The mage drew himself up, hands curling at his side. Cary was ready, would protect Jaime with his life if need be, just to spite this demon.

"Tomorrow, Mr. Robb," Sandover purred, relaxing his fingers. "Until then, he's all yours."

He refused to let go of Jaime, holding him on his lap in the canoe as they returned to the island at legendary speeds. He brought Jaime to the fire, where Patrice promised to keep him safe while Cary ran to the tent to retrieve his tobacco pouch. While Patrice held Jaime upright, Cary cast a generous pinch of heat-bearing yellowsand onto the fire, wafting the smoke towards them with a fan of pine needles.

"Did you put another branch on?" Patrice asked, his face reddening as the yellowsand's smoke rose around him.

"It's my doing. I can't let him die."

"If he's got the deep chill, you gotta get him into bed and get in with him."

"This'll do."

He settled beside the fire and took Jaime in his arms again. Patrice had slipped off the log where he'd been sitting and let his head fall back. Soon he was snoring, a comforting human sound in the aftermath of the otherworldly. Cary shuddered at the memory of those writhing, snakelike tendrils, their gruesome seeking mouths.

He relaxed his desperate grip as Jaime stirred, whimpering softly. This one small, sorrowful man against a monster: Sandover was out of his mind. The duke as well, for trusting a man like Sandover. Ready money said the wretch turned belly up the first sign of real danger. Cary was...not ready to face danger, but willing, if he could know it would be for the better. He'd done enough wrong that if he died doing right, it'd be a fair go.

Evening fell and still he sat by the fire, still Jaime shivered, still Cary's heart ached. He ate what was given, clumsily holding the bowl with one hand, drinking the broth and picking out the chunks of salt-pork and fish with his teeth as he couldn't bring himself to let go of Jaime.

"I tell you, there's only one thing for it," Patrice said as Cary chafed Jaime's pallid hand between his, willing the warmth into him.

"He doesn't like to be touched."

"You're touching him right now, aren't ya? I know I'm not best at the thinking game, but I know how not to die from being alive out here, and if he's got the big chill, you gotta heat it out of him."

He had nothing to lose. Patrice helped carry Jaime to the tent, where he roused enough to crawl in unaided. Cary helped him get into their bedroll, then he peeled off his own damp clothes and got in beside him. Usually they did their best not to brush up against each other, but tonight he curled himself around Jaime's shivering form and willed his warmth into the other man. At last Jaime ceased to tremble. His legs uncurled from his chest and he began to breathe evenly.

"Tell me of the Deathless Duke," he murmured when Cary thought he'd already fallen asleep.

"You don't want to know."

"I do. I don't want to die without knowing something of why."

"What does it matter?"

"I don't know. But I'm too frightened to sleep. Tell me a story. Tell me what happened to you."

"Not sure you're going to want to know that either."

COMRADES

He was born of two worlds. Mum was a Yolngu beauty, a dancer. Dad was a ranger, son of an officer, forbidden to love her. His mother's hands, his father's eyes, his skin a blend of both, just pale enough that he'd pass in a bind if he spoke English carefully.

His hands had always been strong. Skilled. Gifted, his aunties said, his hands made to tell stories, to dip into the stream of dreaming and bring the mysteries into being.

Not strong enough to stop his family from being dispersed. Without his size, he'd have had nothing at all, but shoulders like this matched to hands like these found work as a roustabout, managing the sheep round shearing time. A brutal job, paid half what it was worth, his thick nose and wooly brow enough sign of his Yolngu heritage to keep him from rising to anything better.

And so he accepted his lot. Made himself the best in his benighted class, until his strength and his calm themselves became a threat, until his mere existence made other men—white men—nervous.

A slur. A fight. A lie, and the man who lied was English-born, and so Cary was given a choice. Prison then the curtailed life of a man who'd done hard time, or obedience.

"They gave me a notebook and a heavy stick and a badge with a number on it. Called me a corrections officer. Fancy way of saying bounty hunter. I went where they sent me and took in who they wanted, and if I did a lot of damage in the taking, it was in service of the law. But it made me sick to my stomach. Most of the runaways I brought it shouldn't have been in prison to start with. It's one thing to bring in a bushranger who'd been robbing mail coaches. It's another to track down a man you used to know, put him in irons and throw him in jail, all because he stole a side of bacon from a farmer's wife to keep his family from starving."

"That's why you took work as a guide instead," Jaime said.

"It felt cleaner," Cary replied in the same soft drone in which he'd told his story. "Instead I brought the poison with me."

"You've come here to make amends."

His voice dropped, the subterranean grind of stone on stone. "And yet look what I've done to you."

"You've kept me safe."

"I should have let you get away. No, I should have *made* you go."

"You had good cause not to."

"Are you trying to forgive me?"

Jaime rolled to face him though he could no more see Cary in the dark tent than on any other night. "I already have. This is more. This is me wishing you'd forgive yourself."

"What's the good in that?"

"I'd ask what's the good in carrying around all that weight. If you wish to be kinder in life, you might practice by being kinder to yourself."

"Hm." He fell silent, save for the gentle wheeze of his breath. The crew had turned in and the night was very still, and it occurred to Jaime that he had never shared a bed with another soul until knowing Cary.

Not even in hospital, though other patients had endured all manner of indignities in the crowded wards. Perhaps his mother had held him while he was a babe, before her death at sea. A death he'd been told was impossible.

"You still cold?" Cary murmured when Jaime shuddered.

"No. Just...sad."

"Don't pity me."

"I have none to spare from pitying myself. Cary, I don't want to die here. Not for that spiteful shit Sandover."

"I won't let that happen."

"It might not be up to you."

"Jaime...what did you see down there?"

"Of the creature? Very little. I was too busy swimming for my life."

"We ought to feed it you-know-who," Cary murmured, and it sounded like he was smiling.

"Be our luck it'd spit him out."

"Reckon he's nothing but skin and bones under all that lace and lavender."

"And bile, don't forget the bile."

Biting back a laugh, Cary snorted, and then Jaime could not help himself, and they laughed as quietly as they could until his stomach ached. Despite the day, despite the cold and the danger they faced tomorrow. Comrades in arms, sent to martyr themselves for some grand cause.

"Bless you, Cary. I count on you more than you know."

"What's that mean?"

"I've had so few friends in life. I've learned not to rely on anyone. You can only be betrayed so many times before it's not worth the bother."

"Jaime..."

"Hush. Just know that you're my friend. I have faith in you. I know you'll do all you can to protect me."

"I will."

"I know. I know you will."

"You're the bright star on my horizon. The one good thing left in my life. I won't let you down."

The morning dew had scarcely dried from the grass when Sandover ordered them back to the lake. Midday had done little to warm the water, so Jaime supposed it made no difference when he dove.

"Too bad we got no bear grease," Patrice said, trailing his paddle to turn the canoe.

"To feed that thing?"

"No, for you. That's what I heard, get all greasy before you get in, so the water doesn't stick to you so."

"And that works?"

"Beats me. I hate swimming." Whistling a snatch of song, he resumed paddling.

Jaime peered over the side of the canoe. Summoning the repelling energy he had used to stay dry in the rain, he dipped his fingers into the water. Drew it out again, the droplets beading on his skin but not wetting it. Emboldened, he knelt on the board and dipped his whole hand in then withdrew it: nothing, his skin dry to the touch and glassy feeling. If he could sustain that across his whole body he'd stay much warmer.

Sandover was resplendent in pale green, his tricorn sporting a preposterous plume which kept striking other people in the face. He minced across the raft to where Jaime was disrobing. "*Alors*, Mr. Skye, have you recovered your senses sufficiently to speak of yesterday?"

The air seemed to thicken as Cary stepped nearer, glaring at Sandover as though he hoped he'd catch fire. Jaime wished much the same.

"I was following the edge of this platform we're moored on when I came to a gap," he told Sandover. "A crevice in the rocks, quite deep. I smelled something like that thing of Eckhart's—"

"You are able to smell underwater?"

"So it seems. I decided to come back, and when I swam past the crevice again, something was stirring in the bottom.

"What did you see?"

A stream of noxious bubbles, a pale, reaching arm, an explosive splash and an echoing undersea wave that had blown him to the surface. "I don't know. Things happened very quickly. It was churning the water terribly. I really had no thought but getting back to the raft." Yet here he was, about to face the monster again.

"You will descend this crevice," Sandover said with a pointed smile. "I wish to know what it was you saw."

Dressed down to his shirt, another of the glowing spheres in its harness slung around his chest, Jaime stood at the edge of the raft and thought of that same subtle shield spreading up his hands, his arms, across his shoulders and down his back. Up his spine and around his forehead and down, a slow prickling heat which built across his skin until his whole body glistened with glassine shimmer.

"You right?" Cary asked, appearing beside him. "What've you done to your skin?"

"Can you see it?"

"*I* can. Dunno about them. What is it?"

"A substitute for bear grease."

Giddy, he grinned at Cary then boldly stepped clear of the edge of the raft and dropped into the water. He swam forward at once to not pop up under the raft. The cold didn't nip so fiercely as yesterday, and with something approaching optimism he struck out for the crevice, the bubbles of his last breath streaming behind him.

Enveloped in the shimmering field, he glided sleekly through the water, the pressure diffused, as if a soft, heavy blanket surrounded him. Sooner than expected he had reached the crevice. A good six feet wide at the top, the ridged limestone walls narrowed as they dropped.

Clumps of half rotted weed washed back and forth on the rocky plateaus to either side of the gap. The smell was worse than yesterday even through the energetic field. Jaime sank lower, until he floated just above the rocks. Rather than the usual growth of small plants, the flights of minnows he had seen nearer the raft, the rocks here were covered in bones. Mainly the tiny bones of fish, here and there the skull of a bird or the remains of a small animal.

His eagerness waning rapidly, he approached the gap with care, jerking back as a stream of tiny bubbles came swirling from below. One of the clots of blackish-brown weed had been carried closer by the gentle rock of the water, a different push and pull than the insistent suck of ocean waves.

The clump was the size of a dinner plate, with long pulpy tendrils that swayed above a mat of lesser leaves. As the water carried it even closer he kicked upwards to let it roll past rather than have it flop against his leg. The wake of his movement stirred the pulpy fronds, which stiffened like the trembling leaves of a touch-me-not plant. Except this was no plant, as the pulpy appendages abruptly lay flat, exposing a fleshy mouth-like slit surrounded by a ring of coiled, snakelike arms.

If there was breath in his lungs he would have screamed aloud. He kicked up harder, his horror multiplying as he surveyed the swarm converging on the place he had been. The same creatures he'd seen at Eckhart's, in that drawing of the tentacle beast's larvae.

One of the nearer now levered its crawling body off the rock, winnowing through the water briefly as if leaping at him. Sandover be damned, Cary be spared, but Jaime wasn't going any nearer that—

Fixated by the peculiar creatures swarming over the rock, he had turned his back on the crevice, and so he never saw what it was that grabbed him. Only knew that he was suddenly being dragged violently by a crushing grip around his right ankle, the cold weight of the water collapsing upon him as his spell fell apart.

WHAT WAITS BELOW

The sun shone brightly on the rippling water, a flock of little clouds grazing the southern horizon, the silvery leaves of the poplars on the shore winking in the gentle breeze, and Cary had never felt worse. "What I wouldn't give to know what's going on down there," he muttered.

"You want us to go take a look?" asked Patrice.

"How?"

"I don't mean go down, but maybe I can see him from the boat." Better than nothing, so Patrice and young Coyne boarded a canoe and set off in the direction Jaime had swum. They were perhaps two hundred yards away when Patrice shouted. His legs splayed, he stood up, fighting whatever had a hold of the blade of his paddle.

"*Sacre bleu de...*" Gordo groaned. He cupped his hands round his mouth and shouted. "Patrice, let 'em have the damned paddle!"

Patrice let go, nearly tumbling over the other side of the canoe as the creature flung the paddle away. Tumbling end over end in a tremendous arc, it landed with a faint splash, too far away to be seen. Meanwhile Coyne had begun paddling backwards, stabbing at the water to either side of the canoe to straighten their course as the long canoe yawed back and forth on the choppy water.

Further away, the curving wake of a tentacle cut the surface as the creature threw something large away from itself with violence. An odd way to hunt if that's what it was doing, to toss away your prey, where it could drift anywhere. Or were there other beasts, its offspring perhaps, waiting to be fed the way a bird fed its helpless young?

His stomach knotting, Cary dropped to one knee, splaying his hands on the coarse boards as his astral being sought the comfort of the bedrock beneath the waves. Jaime Skye was down there still, and it was Cary's job to find him. Keep him safe. Keep him alive, not to serve Sandover and the duke's deranged purposes but because Jaime deserved to live.

The creature had ceased thrashing about by the time Patrice and Coyne reached the raft. "Dunno what to tell you, ami," Patrice said to Cary as he clambered aboard. "Except that I wish to the good lord we could all bugger off out of here."

Sandover snapped his gold watch closed and thrust it the fob pocket at the waist of his silk breeches. "You care to repeat that, Monsieur Patrice?"

"You heard me, so...no."

"That's not the point, you cretin."

"I know what that means, Lord Sand-bagger."

"My name is Sandover!"

"So? My name is take me the goddamn home, I don't want to be out here with the flies and the skeeters and the I don't know what the goddamn that thing is," and he made an obscene gesture at the sparkling water. "I was paid to port your lordship out here, not to get mother of Christ killed hunting goddamn lake snakes."

"You were paid to obey."

"*Tais-toi*, I ain't been paid at all nothing yet." Sandover spat a French insult that made every head turn. "*Oh la*," said Patrice, grinning savagely. "*Tu veux aller, violette?*"

And that was that, as the two men launched into battle, screaming and spitting and flapping their hands at one another, their French dialects so unalike as to be different languages. Cary measured the rudeness at each escalation by the growing shock upon Gordo's face. None of which was getting Jaime found.

Undrownable: what did that mean? As long as he was conscious? As long as some working of his held? No ordinary man would still be living if he'd been in the water so long.

Retreating from the dueling pitch, he came across Coyne and the other lad Tench, who were watching with their mouths dangling open. "Can the pair of you pilot one of these?" he asked, nodding to the canoes tethered nearby.

"Back to camp?" Coyne asked hopefully.

"Afraid not. We've got to look for Mr. Skye."

It was not much past midday when they set out. The sun was starting to drop and still they scoured the lake, cutting back and forth in an ever widening arc. Did bodies sink or float? Had he survived the monster's attack? Was he even now clambering out of the water onto the shore, and Cary's wrenching agony was all for nothing?

"Mr. Robb," piped Coyne, pointing with his paddle. "I see something."

He saw it too, a pale form bobbing off the port side. They paddled towards it, Cary holding onto the gunwales as the canoe fought against the choppy surface, for the wind had risen as the day passed.

Little by little, they gained on it, until there was no doubt. He floated face-down, his shirt washing around him, Sandover's glass light extinguished. Cary held his breath as they drew alongside. Tench used the gaff to draw the body nearer, and Cary helped him to pull Jaime from the water. He sat heavily missing the bench and ending on the floor of the canoe, the bilge water soaking through his trousers, Jaime's limp body cradled in his arms.

"That's too bad, Mr. Robb," Coyne said.

"He's not dead."

"It's been hours, but. What hope can there be?"

"He's no ordinary man." He could feel the life in Jaime, the slow thrum of his pulse. Recalling the aftermath of yesterday's dive, he turned Jaime so that he lay forward over Cary's arm, his chest against the gunwales. Sending a desperate plea to his ancestors, to all the gods, to whatever angel had kept this miraculous man alive thus far, he slapped Jaime between the shoulderblades.

A violent shudder wracked Jaime's body as he vomited over the side of the canoe. Cary held him carefully, murmuring encouragement as Jaime brought up all the water he'd taken in. At least he lived, the relief so strong Cary hardly minded as Jaime wiped his soiled mouth on Cary's sleeve.

"Sorry," he mumbled, shoving his smeared, sweating face against Cary's chest.

"No worries. I've got you."

He waved to the people on the raft as they passed, but they did not stop to explain. Once on dry land, Cary went directly to the tent. Jaime was shivering so hard Cary struggled to divest him of his wet shirt. He shoved Jaime inside the bedroll then mixed up the last precious grains of yellowsand with a lump of grease to form a salve. He smeared this over Jaime's hollowed chest then covered it with a sheaf of corkwood bark.

"I'll be right back," he muttered, a promise to himself as much as to Jaime, who was barely sensate, his head flopping from side to side, his hands pawing weakly at the dressing on his chest. Cary covered this with the blanket then crawled out of the tent.

The sun was setting, filtering through the trees, its golden light laying in long bands across the campground. The duke's man had joined the crew at the fire, his presence damping the boys usual glee, yet as Cary surveyed their blank, unfeeling faces he was struck by another more sinister possibility.

Sandover drew near, his eyes glassy, his hand outstretched. "Mr. Robb," he intoned dully. "I do hope our friend Mr. Skye is prepared for his next descent."

As he reached out blindly Cary stepped back. "How dare you call him *friend*? You won't rest until he dies."

"Au contraire, Mr. Robb," Sandover slurred, his pale irises mere bands of icy blue around the depthless black of his eyes. his voice deadened by the enchantment gripping them all. "I want him to live as long as possible. I need him. Even more than you do."

The men seated round the fire had hardly blinked. Cary licked his lips, tasting the sharp chemical aroma overlaying the ordinary scents of charcoal and hot sap. The duke's man sat on the opposite side of the fire, and it was from him that the smoke was coming, trickling from beneath his high-buttoned coat and drifting along the ground.

Cary stepped back, exhaling a steady stream of the tainted air. "As long as I'm alive, Jaime Skye is under my protection," he declared.

"So mote it be," Sandover said, sealing the oath.

Breathing shallowly to avoid breathing any more of the poison, Cary backed away from the fire, his heart heavy with the knowledge that he was now their last defense.

CARY'S REMORSE

For untold hours Jaime floated in a feverish half-dream, pain coming in waves then subsiding as he drifted into deeper sleep. His leg ached, and this is what most often woke him. Every time, Cary was there, to dry his sweating face and throat, to help him bring up more water from his lungs, burning through his apothecary of sacred soil and herbs to save him. Jaime could not stop shivering, his skin pallid and swollen like a drowned corpse, his movements lethargic as if he was still underwater.

He was awakened by a ravenous hunger. Daylight filtered through greyly through the tent walls. Cary was sitting beside him, legs crossed, eyes closed, reminding Jaime of another man who'd saved his life. As he tried to speak Cary stirred. He helped Jaime sit up.

"What do you need?"

"Eat," he croaked, his throat like sandpaper. Cary had a bark cup of softened cooked pemmican and another of wild strawberries. The little teardrop-shaped berries tasted strongly of pine but were soft, dissolving on Jaime's tongue as he ate them one by one.

"When did you pick these?" he asked, for Cary had not seemed to leave him.

"Tench brought me them."

"Since when..." He paused for a bout of coughing that left his lungs feeling wrung out. "Since when did he do your bidding?"

"He offered."

"Hm." He took another berry, his arm leaden. Pressing it to a pulp against the roof of his mouth, he closed his eyes, marveling at the complexity of tastes contained by one tiny fruit.

"Swallow what's in your mouth before it chokes you in your sleep," Cary said as Jaime wriggled under the blankets again.

Thank you, my friend...

This cycle repeated a few times until Cary deemed him well enough to leave the tent. Which Jaime was aching to do, having exhausted his tolerance for staring at dirty canvas.

"How did you keep him away from me?" he asked as he gingerly fit his swollen ankle into his boot. Him meaning Sandover, who had to have taken the last four days of inactivity hard.

"It hasn't been easy," Cary muttered. He had barely spoken since Jaime woke, sitting with his head hanging between his stiff shoulders, his clasped hands shaking. Delicate hands for a man of his size. No, not delicate, with the length of his fingers, the bulge of his knuckles. More, that they were devices of great precision. Strength, precision, magic, and still his hands shook.

"Cary, what is it?"

"He's put a spell on them. They had a fight while you were down there. Him and Patrice. I don't know what went on after cause I was looking after you. But now…it's uncanny." He crawled to the tent flap and opened it a crack. Squinting, Jaime saw the crew sitting around the fire, not one of them speaking or moving. An abnormal quiet, unbroken by birdsong, even the constant susurration of leaves deadened.

"I don't know what he's up to," Cary breathed, "but I don't want it catching you."

"Me neither."

"I can't believe I let this happen," he said, letting the tent flap fall closed.

"How could you have stopped it?"

"Dunno. Hucked his nibs in the sea?"

"You needed him alive."

"At what price? How many more lives am I going to destroy?"

"Are you done playing the martyr?"

Cary raised his head, his expression fearsome. Jaime had learned to see past it to the pain it concealed. "Neither of us asked for this," he said. "But if this is what I have to do to bring you peace, so be it."

"You don't," Cary grunted, lurching towards him as he reached to pull open the tent flap. "Don't do this for me. I've done you nothing but harm."

"Not so. I'd not have survived without you."

"You'd not be here if I hadn't snatched you off the dock back in Portsmouth."

"If it hadn't been you, it would have been another of his puppets. Someone else Sandover and that duke of his connived into their foul games. Or worse, someone as venal as them. Cary, I can't fault you for being caught in the same trap as me, and I can't survive this without you. I want to bring this to an end, but I need to know that you trust me."

"I do. Only you." For all Cary's strength, he teetered on the edge of panic, his hands trembling, his eyes full of sorrow.

"I'm so sorry for all you've gone through, my friend." Jaime set his slim hand over Cary's—larger, coarser—and tried to summon a little of that healing golden light of Adrian's, that blessed sense of peace, his own heart easing as Cary's stiff face softened, his hand no longer trembling so hard.

"To bring you back safe I'd do it again. You're the best thing in my world, Jaime. I won't let you go."

Before leaving the tent, Cary gave him some grease mixed with one of his powders to rub under his nose. The acrid scent made him shudder, like a sharp nail dragging across his scalp.

"Once we get out there it won't be so peaky," Cary said, dabbing it around his own nostrils.

"Fighting fire with fire?"

He didn't reply, only held open the tent for Jaime to scoot through. His ankle still pained him, and he accepted Cary's help to get to his feet. At once he smelled the enchantment in the air, the sickly sweet aroma showing Sandover's hand in the working. The mage could be seen at the shore, in the midst of directing the others to load the last and largest crate onto a canoe. A procedure which on other days would have been marked by the boys' idle chatter and jokes, now and then a working song, but which today passed in silence.

"What's been going on?" Jaime asked as they set out across the beaten earth of the campsite, him at a pitiful limp.

"Dunno," Cary grumbled. "Hard to get a word out of anyone."

As they neared the fire, the duke's man turned towards them. Only his head, pivoting on his shadowy neck, his unmemorable body remaining stock still. No one else noticed them, even Sandover working under the compulsion of a spell. His fine suit of yellow silk was a ruin, daubed from knee to neck with smears of greenish muck, the lace at his cuffs and collar wadded into filthy clumps like the pulpy fronds of those vile black spawn that had swarmed Jaime on the last dive. He caught sight of them at last and stumbled towards them, his heels slipping on the rocks, his gaze unfocused.

"Ah, Mr. Skye. How good of you to join us," he said, the words falling flatly, his jaw flapping like a wooden puppet's.

"What's in the box?" Cary grunted. Sandover swiveled his head towards him.

"*Une surprise,*" he intoned through his slack lips. "For our underwater friend. We're going to widen his front door."

THE BOMB

As the boys hoisted the crate between them and started down the shingle, Sandover joined the duke's man at the fire. They stared at each other for nearly a minute without Sandover saying a word. Suddenly he flinched, like a man who has woken up not in his bed but in an armchair in his study. He glanced down at himself and gasped in horror.

"*Mon Dieu...*" he moaned, spreading his arms wide to regard his sodden lace cuffs and muddy stockings. He started for his tent, then froze, one foot in the air. Wearing his smarmiest smile, he turned back to the duke's man and gestured to his filthy suit.

"Must I really endure this?" he said through his teeth. "At my moment of triumph?" Nothing changed about the duke's man, not in pose or expression, yet his raw frustration at having aligned himself with this Narcissus hung in the air, an elemental tang that made both Cary and Jaime recoil.

"He's getting away with it?" Jaime muttered, as Sandover began backing away from the duke's man, bowing all the while.

"Who bloody cares, that's another hour wasted between now and God knows what."

Loading the crates into the canoes was easy when done from a jetty, and a struggle when done without. Wiry young Coyne was carrying a corner of the cumbersome box, his face as blank as the rest. Shuffling sideways, his heel caught on something and he fell backwards with a splash. The corner dipped towards the water but as Cary strode forward to grab it Cesar stepped in front of him, stopping him with a hard hand against his sternum, his glassy eyes staring straight through him.

"Only trying to help," Cary grunted. He joined Skye where he sat on a shelf of rock jutting from the shore, his boots hanging from his neck by their laces and his swollen ankle in the water. Cesar's touch lingered hotly on Cary's chest, and he resisted the urge to open his shirt and see if he bore a mark. Knowing wouldn't bring him comfort, only remind him that Sandover still owned him.

Coyne got to his feet, his wet hair plastered across his rubbery face, and resumed his position at the corner of the crate. Sandover returned as they were lashing it to the centre seat of the canoe. He was wearing his poncy pink suit, his even brighter pink stockings clocked with a design of serpents and lilies, a cloth-of-silver cloak dripping from his padded shoulders. Cary had seen more modesty at a fancy dress masquerade.

"When does Sir Thomas arrive to take his lordship's portrait?" Jaime murmured.

"Let's hope that thing mistakes him for a worm."

In the tense, wordless shuffle that followed he got separated from Jaime, who ended up in the same canoe as Sandover. By the time he reached the raft Cary was shaking worse than ever. He knew the risks of abusing his craft, of relying on smoke to make up for a lack of astral strength, and he was starting to feel the consequences of going without.

Blunted by the enchantment that had sapped their will, the others were little help as he gathered himself to make the broad step from the canoe to the raft. Even Gordo stood dumbly as the tail of the canoe swung wide when yesterday he would have cursed and reached for the gaff.

Never had Cary been so grateful for the post erected at the centre of the raft. In the hours of waiting for Jaime to wake, he'd knotted a harness that tied around his shoulders and chest and braided a sturdier rope that he now bound to the post. He nearly fell as the raft pivoted suddenly, for Gordo was raising one of the anchors.

Jaime had boarded and joined him, his face pale. "What's his purpose in setting us adrift?" he asked, bending his knees as the raft pivoted in the opposite direction.

"I don't think that's what he's after," Cary replied as he felt the tug. Patrice and Coyne had remained in the canoe and were now towing the raft westward towards the gap in the stone underfooting of the island. Towards the beast.

The nearer they got to the crevice, the worse for Jaime. The poor bloke was beside himself, his breath quick and panicked, his face clammy beneath his summer tan as he clung to Cary's arm.

"I don't want to go down there," he muttered.

"I don't want you to go."

"It's too late to stop this, isn't it?"

Perhaps his talent and Jaime's together was enough to overcome Sandover but was that enough to get them free? He glanced back at the island, at the black clad figure with the moon-pale face lingering on the shore, who he shouldn't have been able to see so clearly. Like the uncanny bloke was just a few yards away. Or lodged in his mind.

They weighed anchor no more than fifty yards from the underwater crevice, marked by a break in the shoreline. From the centre of the raft it was impossible to see down into the water so Jaime ventured to the edge. He returned, his face paler than ever.

"Those black spawn have spread, or bred, or I don't know," he said miserably, rubbing his arms. "Whatever happened, there's hundreds of them, all over the rocks." He flinched, pressing himself against Cary as the sides of the crate fell to the deck of the raft with a thud.

The object inside was wrapped with straw and wadded cotton. Sandover himself peeled this back to reveal a black iron ball two hands wide. Long nails protruded from its surface in a regular placement, reminding Cary of the prickly sea urchins he'd seen in the shallows off Kalimantan.

Jaime flinched again, his eyes flying open. "Dear God...it's a bomb."

"How do you know?"

"Just a guess, but I've seen enough machinery in my time at the patent bureau. Every now and then we'd get an application that we'd forward directly to the Home Office, to keep fools from building lethal devices in the back garden. I'll warrant those rods are triggers."

"How's he going to set it off underwater? No flint will light wet powder."

"What if he has a tinderbox like Strike's? Or some other trickery?"

"Safe to assume so."

Jaime cast a sad look back towards the camp. "I rather wish I'd stayed in the tent."

"You and me both."

As plans went, it was as good as they might expect, given that most of the crew were enchanted and their master was out of his mind. The bomb relied on clockwork. The powder sat in the central chamber, the protruding rods acting as flints, letting off sparks when scraped against the inner surface of their shafts by the spring-wound gears. "It *should* work," Jaime murmured to Cary as the others wrestled the spiny sphere into the water. "I've granted patents to less feasible machinery. Still..."

"Careless butchery and nothing more," Cary grunted.

"Aye."

"Wish we'd let that Strike bloke have at him."

"There's that as well. Faith, there's no chance we'll survive this, is there?"

"We will."

"If not," Jaime said with a hitch in his voice, "know that I did all I could for you."

"I know. I won't let him destroy us."

He bowed his head. "I want to believe that's enough. Your words. Your will."

"You're under my protection. You belong with me. He can never destroy that."

Jaime looked up, his eyes bright with emotion. "You're right. Thank you, friend."

"Save it. We've got a ways to go before you should be thanking me."

After a bitter stand-off which culminated in Sandover threatening to set fire to the raft, Tench drew the short straw. Blubbering, he slithered into the canoe and approached the bomb which hung tethered between it and the other canoe. Under Sandover's increasingly terse instructions, Tench unscrewed the cover from a hand-sized hole on the upper surface of the bomb, then wound the mechanism inside, nearly dropping the cover in his haste to screw it back on as a loud ticking commenced. The others boarded the canoes and they struck out, towing the bomb.

When they reached the gap, one canoe kept on while the other turned about, playing out the rope to keep the device from striking bottom. Then with the bomb poised over the crevice, the ropes were cut. As it began to sink the canoes took off, paddling like mad in opposite directions to not be caught in the blast.

The blast which never came, the raft rocking gently on the calm water, Sandover checking his fob watch again and again as if that alone could bring it about. "Tell me, your lordship," Jaime said acidly after close to half an hour had passed. "What was it you did to this duke of yours to be punished with this task?"

"*Pardon*?" Sandover hissed, his hand going to the hilt of his short sword, which was perhaps not the fussy encumbrance it had seemed.

"I mean, was this really your plan?" Jaime went on, a reckless light in his eyes as he gestured at the undisturbed water, the empty crate, the entranced crew standing by stiffly. "We've dragged this lump of iron across the sea, up hill and down dale and all the way out to the middle of this damned lake for you to fail to blow up some rocks? Or is his grace perhaps using this idiotic quest as a pretense to rid himself of an irritating lord magister?"

"Question me again," Sandover grated through his bared teeth. "And I shall kill you where you stand."

"What's the damned difference?" Jaime spat. "It's you killing me either way. Might as well get on with it. Save me the suspense."

"If you insist." Sandover threw his hands towards Jaime, sending a hot blast of radiant force across the deck and sweeping him into the water. Cary surged to his feet but fell back as a scorching pain shot through him, setting his bones alight. It ended just as suddenly, leaving him curled on himself, his lips bleeding where he'd bit them to keep from screaming his guts out.

"Damn you, leave him be!" Jamie cried, out of sight below the angle of the deck.

"Or what?" Sandover said with a pursed smile. A smile which split into a soundless shriek, his whole body shaking as his face went a violent shade of red to rival his suit. He dropped to his knees, heaving for breath.

"Can't take your own medicine, you coward?" Jaime cried with a note of triumph.

"How dare you!" Snarling, Sandover wrenched himself to his feet. Snatching a short knife from his belt, he leapt at Cary who still reeled from his earlier assault. Straddling him, he pressed the point of the blade to the soft skin behind Cary's ear.

"You managed to defeat my hypnosis," he purred. "This does not surprise me. Cherish that victory, Mr. Robb. It shall be your last."

RUIN

Jaime didn't like how quiet it was. Aboard the raft, the boys were as lively as posts, standing mutely, their heads listing awkwardly on their necks. The creature's offspring massing beneath him in their hundreds couldn't be heard, though he could sense their undulating movements even through his clinging clothes, the black polyps smothering the rock in all directions.

Sandover reappeared, smiling too broadly. He was holding a glittering blade to Cary's throat, his other hand knotted in Cary's thick hair as he drove him on hands and knees towards the edge of the raft.

"Do you know what a hydra is, Mr. Skye?" he crowed.

"A myth."

"If so, then the tale has more than a little truth to it."

"That *thing* down there is not a damned hydra!"

"Yet for every one of those arms you cut away, another grows," Sandover replied. "And the part you cut away will seed itself anew. It is unkillable. Like myself. And unlike him." Cary tensed, his face blank with terror, as Sandover pressed the blade against his skin.

"Leave him alone!"

"You don't give the orders, *piece du merde*," Sandover hissed. "You will do as I tell you or watch him die. Now take a rock or a stick or your own stubborn head and throw it at that bomb until it ignites."

"You're a madman!"

"And yet it is you who has spent half his life in the asylum."

"Because of a lie. You let him alone or I shan't do what you want. I'll let that monster have me, tear me to bits, so you can go back to your master and tell him you failed. You can join him in hell!"

He was losing control, the sky darkening above them, the waves rising. Or was that his weapon, as the wind snatched Sandover's obscene hat from his head. Vain to the last, he let go of Cary to grab for it, stopping short of falling off the raft as the hat went sailing across the water.

A short lived victory as something huge and heavy struck the water behind Jaime, drenching him. As Cary shouted a warning he turned to see a writhing red tentacle burst from the water. It whipped through the air and slammed down on the surface, sending another wave over Jaime's head and making the raft dip and bob.

"The bomb!" Cary yelled as the others went reeling across the pitching deck. "That thing will set it off any second." The next moment the creature's foot-thick limb caught Jaime around the middle and sent him flying.

The hard landing knocked the breath from his lungs. Who needed breath? Not a waterman, and rather than fight the choppy waves he sunk beneath the surface a few feet. He had landed far from the island, beyond the protective shelf of bedrock that held up the island, and he wriggled out of his heavy jacket and let it fall into the inky depths.

The black spawn had spread down the face of the underwater cliff, more of the squirming, writhing beasts emerging from the crevice where the mother made its home. It was moving, its shapeless grey-pink body rising up the shadowy crevice, its arms with their hideous seeking mouths churning the water in search of something to latch onto. Higher it climbed, closer and closer to the spiny egg of the bomb, which sat on a ledge several feet below the edge of the gap, balanced precariously on some unseen outcropping of rock. At any second now it might ignite, by the creature's flailing limbs or one of its swarming spawn.

Why had he and Cary not formed a plan? Stolen a canoe, left the others to their fate. The boys' own fault for taking money from a madman, but even as he thought this he knew that if he did nothing to prevent their deaths, they would haunt him until his own.

Angling away from the break in the underwater cliff, he struck out towards the raft. The hideous spawn were massing beneath it, centred on the pair of ropes which tethered it to the stone anchors. Without warning the raft began to pitch back and forth, foaming the water and scattering the black spawn with the backwash. Jaime kicked to the surface to see Cary and Sandover locked in battle.

Neither had the advantage. Sandover's coat was singed and smoking in several places, his long hair snaking about his face. Cary had dropped to one knee, a torsioning plane of lucent energy suspended between his shaking hands, the lines of force warping the very air as they arced towards Sandover.

The boys lay where they'd fallen, knocked down by the raft's wild motion or by magic. All the while the beast's arms thrashed the water, its blindly seeking mouths coming ever nearer to the raft as it crawled up from the depths of the crevice.

The next events happened nearly on top of one another, the time stretching like taffy as Cary clapped his hands together then slapped them down on the deck of the raft, sending a blast of radiant energy towards Sandover, hurling him backwards as if kicked by a draught horse. The next instant the bomb ignited, sending a vast plume of water rocketing into the sky, followed an second later by a great churning wave that swept over Jaime and send him tumbling head over heels into dark water.

His ears ringing, he righted himself. Or so he thought, but every direction he swam seemed colder and deeper. A bright pink figure suddenly burst diagonally across his field of view, trailing a cloud of shiny bubbles. Sandover, his limbs wheeling, the silver cape and his white-blond hair fanning out around him as he sank.

Orienting himself at last, Jaime struck out towards the sinking figure. Sandover was a wretch, a foul-brained lackey of that demonic duke, but Jaime was not so callous as to let anyone drown before his eyes. Or was it that he wanted Sandover to live a long, unpleasant life in whatever the mages used for a jail?

The pale cliff of rock emerged from the murky water as he neared Sandover, who was struggling with his heavy cloak. Sensing him, the mage looked up with an expression of perfectly human terror, but even as Jaime reached for him a clutch of the black spawn propelled themselves off the cliff face and wrapped themselves around Sandover. A garbled shriek bubbled from his gaping mouth as the weight of the creatures bore him down into the depths.

More of the beasts were flinging themselves at Jaime, their short tentacles whipping about, their hideous beaks snapping. He looked down at fluttering motion beneath him. Borne by the cycling current as it struck the rocky shelf beneath the island and flowed back towards the lake, the monsters were rising, reaching for him, blind and ravenous.

No!

In the past he had asked, clearly if not always patiently, for the water to obey him. In this urgent moment his instinctive terror was enough, and he was suddenly hurtling through the water, driven by a great percussive wave that blew the black spawn against the face of the rocks and sent Jaime hurtling in the opposite direction and into oblivion.

RESCUE

Cary drifted for many hours without sight of land. Even had he trusted himself to manage the canoe lashed to the raft, the beast's arms had smashed a hole in the hull and the vessel was useless. Using Strike's flint, he lit the lodestone candle to get his bearing, then laid on his front dragging a paddle in the water as a sort of rudder, but either he knew too little of sailing or the raft was too heavy to turn.

On and on he went with still nothing around him but water. Fresh water, and he crawled to the edge now and then to drink from his cupped hand. As the sun began to sink below the horizon he lit the candle again, one tiny spark against infinity.

And all for nothing. Jaime was gone. The others dead or drowned or God knew. The monster's horrific spawn was scattered on the current, to infest the rest of the lake. If he had any dignity, he'd walk off the edge of the raft and put an end to everything. Give up trying to absolve himself of the harm he had caused throughout his life. Yet if he died, Jaime's death went unavenged.

And then he heard an engine. Or was that the sound of his own heart as it laboured to keep beating beneath the weight of his sorrow? He got to his feet, clinging to the post. Away to the southwest, a long dark shape set with lights moved beneath a plume of smoke. A steamer? Any vessel would do, and as it grew steadily closer he began to shout, waving his arms to draw someone's eye. Any eye, but even his booming voice was lost in the sound of its churning paddlewheels.

The ship was near enough he could see people walking to and fro on the deck, the lights winking whenever someone passed in front of them. He'd snuffed the candle to preserve it, and now lit it again. As he shouted he passed his hand in front of the light, hoping that someone aboard saw the flickering, but the big ship didn't slow.

His voice growing hoarse, he set the candle on the deck, pulled off his stiff coat and waved it overhead as a flag. A light on the ship began to flicker, a regular blinking like someone opening and closing the shutter of a lantern. He threw down his coat and gingerly picked up the shortened candle in its tin holder, trying to match the pattern of the flicker. Another light on the side of the ship began to drop. As it moved away from the dark mass of the barge the slim shape of a canoe resolved, paddling towards him at speed.

The grizzled man in stained buckskin at the prow of the canoe had Gordo's wandering eyes, Cesar's lank curtain of hair, and Patrice's odor, but he was the dearest thing Cary had ever seen.

"Is there just the one of you?" he asked as Cary huddled on the seat behind him.

"Dunno what's left of the others."

"Is that so? Where've you come from?"

"Misery Bay. I got to get back there."

"That'll have to be on you, I'm sorry to say. I've to stick with the steamer."

"I'll pay you."

He turned to look squarely at Cary. "With what?" he asked softly, his eyes briefly lighting on the fellow piloting the stern of the canoe.

"Do you know what a lodestone candle is?"

His greying brows lifted. "Why, have you got one?"

"It's yours if you'll do as I ask."

"What about him?" he asked with a flick of his eyes to indicate the other fellow.

"Does he happen to like tobacco?"

The purple sky blazed with stars by the time they reached the little cove. "You're certain this is it?" Cary asked, squinting into the darkness, for not a light shone across the campsite, the water lapping softly at the unseen shore.

"Sure as sure I am," said his guide, whose name was Denis, and whose partner had turned out to very much like tobacco. "I know this here island like no one."

"Who's going there?" came a shout.

Denis unshuttered the lantern and swept the light across the grounds. Patrice was splashing towards them across the shingle. The other boys huddled around the unlit fire, but there was no sign of Sandover, or of the duke's clay-faced man. Or of Jaime, but Cary set that aside as Patrice helped him out of the canoe, then clasped him to his chest.

"Goddamn good to see you," he choked, pounding Cary's back.

"Might we get out of the water?" Cary wheezed.

"Why? Oh! Sure thing."

Cary thanked his rescuers then waded onshore, the starlight just bright enough to keep him from stumbling. All five of the boys had made it through the ordeal, though they were a sorry lot, huddled in their wet clothes around the fire which Gordo was struggling to relight.

"Shame about the little fella," he murmured as Cary knelt beside him with Strike's smoldering tinderbox. "He was a fighter, no doubt."

Cary only nodded. He was lucky to be alive. Lucky to only be tired and frightened and not stuck on a raft in a lake the size of the sea. Lucky to have known a man like Jaime, selfless to the last. He tried to thank Gordo, but he had no breath to speak, as if a huge weight bore down on his chest. Pain he knew, and shame, and fear and loneliness, but never such heartbreak, a sense of the world being somehow reduced for no longer containing Jaime Skye.

With the ever-burning tinderbox they woke the fire. Seated on the ground, his back against a log, Cary gnawed a little hardtack and pemmican, but the trials of the day soon caught him up. Rather than huddle alone in the tent he let sleep find him where he was.

He woke feeling as sore in body as he was in spirit. It was punishingly early, no one up but the birds and the dew, and it took him a few tries to get to his feet. He hadn't eaten in a day, hadn't eaten well in a month, and he stopped to hitch up his stained trousers. Never had he longed so badly for the comforts of an ordinary city, where the worst danger was another man's ire and not drowning by lethal creatures or lunatic mage.

He reached the shore and wandered westward along the slabs of dimpled stone, until he reached the break in the shoreline where the underwater crevice lay. He tried to fix the scene in his mind, for he ought to tell Dr Eckhart how to find the creature. If the thing could not be killed it could at least be avoided.

Satisfied that he could describe the area, he was about to head back when he saw a movement in the scrub on the far side of the gap. He froze, searching among the trees, but saw nothing. As he turned once more, a small, dear face beneath a thatch of sun-reddened hair poked out from behind a clump of birch.

"Jaime! Stay put, I'll come get you."

"No, *you* stay put," he shouted back. He darted away through the forest, towards the heart of the island. Cary dithered, for the scrub grew thickly along this strip of shore. He was forced to retrace his steps nearly to the campsite, all the while keeping an eye for Jaime in the forest, for he could not lose him again, could not lose this chance to save them both.

Covering his head with one arm, he shoved through the thicket and gained the more open ground beneath the trees. Still no sign of Jaime, and he was going to start calling his name when he heard a sharp whistle. There between two leafless trunks at the top of a short rise was Jaime Skye, and the wretched tension in Cary's chest dissolved into the greatest joy he'd ever known as his friend, his *heart*, his Jaime came pelting down the little slope and ran to him, shouting with delight, alive, alive.

SIR DEATH

Jaime was not a man who liked to be touched, but today, here, now, he threw himself into Cary's arms and clung to him, immersing himself in the sense of being wanted. Cherished, Cary rocking him like a mother would, murmuring apologies for what he'd endured and prayers to his gods and to Jaime's for their deliverance. Cary, alive and whole and here with him, now and forever.

As they walked back to the campsite shoulder to shoulder Jaime filled the gaps in Cary's knowledge of the events as best as he was able. When he'd regained consciousness on a gravelly spit some five miles to the west, he had lain face down in the wet shoals and prayed to go back to sleep, hopefully forever. Nature had supplied the means of rousing him as his body went through its usual purging of the water he'd taken in. A tiresome business without Cary's aid, but at last he had crawled up the nominal beach and lain down on the first dry flat place he found.

"I woke up with a little Haudenosee child poking me with a stick. When I didn't retaliate, she must have judged me harmless, and led me to her village on Elizabeth Bay, just north of here. Really impressive structures, those longhouses, for a people who choose not to build with stone. England wouldn't have needed so many wars if they hadn't had to keep paying for all those dratted castles."

"That's a leap of logic" Cary chuckled.

"Am I rambling? I'm just so pleased to see you. For my sake and yours." Pleased wasn't the word for it. Restored, revived, blissful even, like a man pardoned on the eve of his execution. He hadn't lost this precious gift, this holy man whose power he had barely begun to understand, who had put his own life second to keep Jaime safe. Later he would ask what had become of Cary's obligation to the duke now that Sandover was gone. Tomorrow, when he had the strength to hear the answer.

"What was it that you did to his nibs while you were in the water?" Cary asked as they came out of the woods onto the rocky shore where the going was easier. "When he had that little fit?"

"Made his blood boil. I think."

"You did something to him, all right."

"I didn't like to do it. That's more power than anyone should have."

"It was him or you."

"Or you. That's what mattered. In the moment I think I could have ripped out his throat with my bare hands if it stopped him from harming you."

"Do you know what happened to him?" Cary said.

"Don't you?"

"Things got a bit frantic. Me and him had squared off, but then the fight just went out of him. He was hissing and spitting, but wouldn't cast. Screaming about blood oaths and prophecies, then one of that thing's arms swept the deck and sent him flying."

"He landed near me, started sinking at once thanks to that silly cape."

"Is he dead?"

"For his sake, I hope so. The black spawn got him."

"He said he was unkillable."

"Yes, his deal with Sir Death. He said a lot of things. Many of which proved meaningless or false. I'm not going to let his soul weigh on mine." More, he wished not to think of how it might feel to be consumed by all those little mouths. Coming out of the woods onto the bare rock of the shore, they both stopped on seeing a pulpy black blob. Other spawn lay along the waterline and must have washed ashore sooner, their tendrils shriveled to reveal their bodies' tripartite shape, curling as they dried into a sort of hollow sphere. One creature had wrapped itself around Sandover's pink and rumpled hat.

They approached the nearest with due caution. Five yards away they paused. The thing hadn't stirred, its finger-like tendrils lying limp and wrinkled, save around its mouth where they had closed in around it like the pursed bud of a thistle. Cary tossed a few pebbles at it to no result. Armed with larger, heavier stones, they drew nearer, but the thing didn't stir.

"So they can't breathe air, that's a relief," Jaime said, tossing aside his stones.

"You can't assume it's dead. I've seed toads buried in the mud six months or more come hopping out good as anything once the Wet started."

"I know one thing," Jaime said as Cary bustled him past the ominous blob. "I won't be happy until we're off this island."

"Begs the question of how."

The fire was burning cheerily when they reached the campsite, a fresh pot of coffee keeping warm on the side, but no sign of the duke's man or of the boys. Sandover's tent stood on its own across the clearing from the rest. A pair of small trunks lay open in front, silk stockings and lace jabots spilling onto the grass. The sound of ripping fabric emerged from the tent, followed by Patrice wearing Sandover's blue coat with the lilies, the sleeves torn off to fit his muscular arms.

"That's better without them big floppy things getting in the way," he said, regarding himself with a grin.

"*For-mi-dable*!" Gordo thrust his way out of the tent, one of Sandover's tricorns mashed onto his sizeable head, the red cloak pinned to the shoulders of his plaid woolen coat.

"You look like one of them muskrateer *gars*, in that book you read me," Patrice said admiringly.

"It's Musketeer, but damned if you aren't right." Thrusting back his shoulders, Gordo struck a heroic pose, his hands on his hips, chin high. Then he spied Jaime and Cary coming towards them. "*Sacre cœur de Jesu*!" he cried, grabbing the brim of his hat in both hands like it might fly away. "Boys, look who's back!"

As well as the two small boxes, Sandover had two large trunks overflowing with his absurd clothes. An ornate wooden secretary inlaid with Sandover's crest in gold lay on the ground. Recalling the cabin boy on the lake barge who had nearly choked after carelessly touching Sandover's goods, Cary brought up a gust of wind to flip open the top, but the case proved to be empty.

"Are you looking for something in particular?" Jaime asked as Cary began rifling Sandover's bedding. Cary grunted in reply and kept searching. Jaime left him to it, for the smell of Sandover in the tent was making his teeth hurt. He joined the others seated about the fire in their new attire.

"What a stroke of luck, eh, boys?" Gordo said. "With all Mr. Fancy Fish Food left behind, we'll make out all right for him not having paid us."

"I may be able to offer you another job," Jaime said, placing his nearly full mug on the ground between his feet, for the tarry coffee had made his hands start shaking with the first sip. "I know someone who may wish to return here and—"

"Nope," Gordo said, flinging up his hand. "Stop yourself and save your breath. No offence, Mr Skye, but this island can go suck eggs."

The party soon broke up, the boys back to the tent to formally divide their plunder. Cary lingered, turning his cup between his hands. "Is that your plan, to come back?" he asked.

"Not if I can help it. But we ought to tell Dr Eckhart. He's the local expert."

"And then?"

"Then home," Jaime said, though the word evoked no sentiment. "I hope. Assuming Mrs Meldrum kept my room for me. Really, I need to see Adrian. I can't imagine he's let this pass."

"You've mentioned him heaps. Who is he?"

"The first person who believed in me." He explained for the first time in detail his friendship with Lord Adrian Lear. A man with power to rival Sandover's, and a heart of purest gold. "If I'd not left him that day in the park, after that horrible interview at Arbitration Hall, none of this might have happened."

"The duke would have found a way," Cary murmured.

"And I might have never found you. So there, if I seek the meaning in this sad venture, it's that it brought us together."

"A steep price to pay to make a man's acquaintance."

"That's not all this is, though, is it? An acquaintance. Tell me, if I said good-bye to you and we went our separate ways—"

"You wouldn't, though."

"No. And I don't want to. You may have talked yourself out of it, but you were right, we are stronger together."

Cary ducked his head, trying to hide his smile. "Sorry for, you know, the kidnapping and all," he mumbled.

"I'm sorry for you. What's going to happen to you?"

"Dunno. The duke's man must have taken everything. Then again, it might not make a difference. They all might have been lying to me from the start."

"If there's anyone who'll know, it's Adrian. And I can't imagine the magisters' assembly as a whole is very pleased with this duke. Regardless of their position, Adrian has both the power and the will to seek justice. And I'd be happy for the company on the way."

"Company?"

"You, Cary. Whatever happens next, I want us to face it together. I'm not going to give up on my best friend."

Not twice in one lifetime. Yet he felt, stronger than ever before, that he would see Adrian again. That these two men were meant to meet, his best and only friends, who had both put themselves in danger to protect him, to whom he owed his life.

After a comfortable night in their dear little tent, they took most of the next day to march the twenty or so miles between Misery Bay and the trading post at Providence Bay. The boys had insisted on bringing the trunks, which made for an arduous journey through forest and sand-marsh, but which paid off handsomely when they were able to trade them for a stout canoe. Of the sort made for long voyages, it fit the seven of them easily now that they didn't have to contend with Sandover or his cargo.

"Tomorrow if we set out good and early we should be able to get youse as far as Fitzwilliam," Gordo said, pointing to the landmarks on the map tacked to the trading house's wall. "Then another day to Dyers, then who knows cause we gotta get around Cape Croker, and—"

"We can't catch a steamer?" Cary grunted, frowning at the map.

"You got money for passage?" Gordo asked him. Cary's brows lowered further, his eyes hooded.

"I might be able to help," Jaime said. "Not with money, just with time."

He put off Gordo's questions. After a much less comfortable night in a creaking iron bed in the only sanitary hotel in the vicinity, a two-storey wooden frame building with a cracked marble bar top and a distinct odor of smoked fish, he joined the crew at the jetty early the next morning. Mist swayed above the softly rippling water, birds trilling from every treetop as they boarded the canoe.

"I'll need to sit there," Jaime said as Cesar went to take his usual place at the prow. The wordless man looked at him hard but did not argue, taking the seat behind Jaime.

He waited until they had left the encircling arms of the little bay and gained open water. Then, feeling terribly self-conscious with every-one's eyes upon his back, he set both hands on the curving wood of the gunwales. He closed his eyes, sending his senses down into the water. The current was in their favour, bearing southeastward, and he let his mind reach further, seeking the peaty tang of the river that had brought them to Georgian Bay.

"Start rowing," he murmured.

"Paddling," Cary grunted from halfway down the canoe.

Jaime smiled didn't reply, his awareness diffusing, dissolving, spreading out through the water, the contour of the lakebed imposing itself on his enchanted senses so it seemed he could feel the shape of the rocks on his tongue, the current's flow mapped to his veins.

As he had when at sea, he did not beg or command the waters. Simply asked: *help us home. We don't belong here and you know it. Take us home, and we will leave you in peace.*

SOUTHBOUND

From the first bite of the paddles Cary knew that Jaime's power was undiminished, as the canoe sliced through the water like an arrow through the air.

"*Jesu*, what's with this thing?" Gordo grunted from the seat behind Cary. "I never did hear of a sideways rip."

"It's Skye," Cary blurted, grabbing for the gunwales as the canoe dipped. "He's calling the current."

"You don't say?"

"Don't drop your paddle."

Jaime had got to his feet, leaning over the prow like a man on a spirited horse. Every dig of the voyageurs' paddles drove them faster, spray bursting from the surface as they skipped across the waves. Cary alternated between a giddy joy at seeing Jaime at his finest, and gripping the gunwales and praying to not be bumped from his seat. They blew through the rocky straights at Tobermory in a matter of minutes, narrowly missing a slow moving steam barge which turned to cross their path.

"A'starbord!" Jaime cried as they shot past the point. Seated ahead of Cary, Tench thrust his paddle into the water. He swore in his frontier French as the paddle was ripped from his hands. The rest fared better, merely dipping their paddles into the furious wake of their passage and leaning into the turn.

Another hour passed at this ludicrous pace, measured by Cary's hard breaths, the tempo of his heart. Jaime stayed on his feet throughout, now and then shouting directions to bear harder left or right. One minute they were ploughing through open water. The next they were racing towards a green and very solid shore, their pace barely slackening as they hurtled through the harbor at Wasaga at impossible speeds, past steamers and sailboats and other canoes, the bells on the harbor buoys clanging their way down the scale as they flew by.

And then they were in the river, the weight of the ground beneath them palpable to Cary's earthy senses. Dry land, even as they drove up the river as if dragged by demons. Here at the sandy mouth the Nottawasaga curved back on itself, and Jaime relinquished control to the boys and their paddles.

Cary longed to go to him, give him a touch of courage. He set his hands on the gunwales and willed his loving care to Jaime through the sinews of the wood. Willed the canoe to hold true, to preserve them, to bear them home. As if sensing his sentiment, Jaime looked back over his shoulder, his smile thin but brave. They had survived, together.

Driven by Jaime's power, they soared up the river against the current at thrice the speed they'd descended. Cary had given up trying to spot landmarks, or even to keep his eyes open, his stomach in active protest against the heaving of the canoe as it skimmed across the water's surface. Just as he was about to beg for amnesty, their speed began to slake and the vessel ceased its rocking, plummeting motion.

He opened his eyes. They were paddling at something like an ordinary pace up the river, the banks a mere dozen feet to either side. In a few minutes more they were drawing up into the shallows at the portage point where they had embarked at the start of this ruinous journey.

"*Sacre Coeur*, boys, that was legendary," Gordo said, holding the canoe steady as the others climbed out. Cesar gestured to Patrice, and the two of them bent over the side of the vessel.

"*C'est vrai*," Patrice said to him. "Looks like we've sprung a leak."

"Here's another," Coyne said, pointing to the stern. "I didn't want to bother you, but."

Between them they dragged the canoe out of the water and up to flatter ground. Several of the pegs holding the canoe's ribs to the sides had shaken loose in their wild race, a distance of some hundred and forty miles. They'd covered it in a matter of a few hours, the last leg against a strong downhill current. As the boys unlashed the tents and other luggage Jaime withdrew to the edge of the forest and sat down clumsily to rest his back against a tree. The ground rocking beneath his unsteady feet, Cary joined him.

"I felt a bit silly standing up there," Jaime said with a weary sigh. "But it worked."

"How are you?"

"Right now or all together?"

"Either."

"I could sleep for about a century. And I'm terribly hungry. But I'm alive. And so are you. So in the balance, I'm happy. I'm happy you're here with me."

They made camp for the night at the head of the portage. The return trip to Barrie passed in a blur, a single uneventful day against the hours of misery they'd endured transporting Sandover's grotty clothes and horrid bomb. The further from the lake, the lighter Cary's heart, for as long as they'd been on open water he'd been plagued by visions of Sandover's corpse rising from the depths, its flesh torn by the savage beaks of the black jellies. Now he was merely plagued by mosquitoes, and not nearly so badly as on the outward journey, for Jaime had learned to spread his repellant energy around him like a cloud, protecting those near him from the worst of the swarms.

Yet more days passed as they travelled southward, some dull, some too adventurous for anyone's liking. At first when they met with crowds Cary kept an eye out for a foppish flash of pink or blue, but by the time they reached the top of Yonge Street he spared no more thought to Sandover, known only to the others by the gruesome moniker Mr. Fancy Fish Food.

They bid farewell to the boys at the Bloor Street toll gate. Following Gordo's anecdotal directions (*turn at the sign with a goose, count three streets, then look for a farrier and turn the other way*) they came at last to the grimy borough where Eckhart and Strike kept their workshop. As on their first visit, one of the wide doors stood open to the courtyard.

As they approached, a fierce blue light flared, bathing the wall of the workshop and glancing off the machinery arrayed across the benches. A pale man in a red velvet frock coat came stumbling backward out of the open door, his coat and long brown hair smoking in several places.

Strike came after, white heat radiating from his raised fists, his work-clothes scorched in long ashy streaks. His eyes flicked to Cary and Jaime. "So you made it back in one piece," he said, not dropping his fists or his gaze. "Maybe you can tell this donkey's backend what happened to his nasty friend."

"If you mean Sandover, he's dead," Jaime said with a cold edge of derision.

The other man whirled about, hatred twisting his otherwise fine features. "You're lying!" he hissed.

"I saw him die," Jaime replied bluntly. "Consumed by the same creatures he was sent to tame."

"Lord Sandover is alive! You will tell me where he is."

"He's at the bottom of a deep lake," Cary said, stepping in front of Jaime as the man advanced. "You can bloody well go and find him yourself."

"Mr. Robb, is it?" said the man in red. "Then this sniveling insect you're so valiantly protecting must be Jaime Skye. I did expect something more from Horatio Skye's son, but as they say, the fortune is lost in the third generation."

"Shut your mouth, Rotherhithe," Strike spat, little bolts of lightning racing up his arms. "You have no business here."

"True. My business is elsewhere." His nose in the air, he passed between Cary and Strike to pick up his tall straw hat from the cobbles. A feint, as he pivoted on his toes and lunged towards them, slipping around Cary to grab Jaime's left arm just below the elbow. Jaime cried out in pain but Rotherhithe had already let go. The next instant the mage was sent spinning across the courtyard as he was struck by a flare of lethal white light.

"That one was for your friend Sandover," Strike said with an ugly smile. "Make sure you give it to him when you see him in hell."

"This isn't over," Rotherhithe hissed. Smoke rising from a newly charred patch on his sleeve, he limped out of the courtyard. A blank-faced man in funerary black waiting in the shadow of the wall across the alley fell into step behind him as he limped away.

"Jaime, did you see that," Cary said. "Jaime? What's happened?" For Jaime was clutching his arm to his chest, his face ashen and streaming with panicky sweat. "What did he do to you?"

"I don't know."

"Say, what did happen to Sandover?" Strike asked as Cary ushered Jaime towards the open workshop door.

"I'll explain in a minute. Can we get him inside?"

AT THE LAST

The stinging pain persisted though his arm showed no mark, and Cary insisted on mixing up a salve. Strike remained in the workshop, cleaning up from the encounter with Rotherhithe. Jaime's mind seethed with questions, but he patiently described the underwater creatures to Eckhart, who made a number of sketches of the parent and of the spawn.

Eventually he asked to stop, his stomach roiling from the pain in his arm and the persistent stench of rot drifting from the specimen room. As Cary smeared his gritty concoction over Jaime's arm, Eckhart put away his pencils in their tin.

"Thank you for telling me," he said. "We'll need to organize a party to investigate."

"Exterminate, more like," said Strike, appearing in the doorway.

"Is that fair?" Cary asked, wiping his sticky fingers on his handkerchief. "It doesn't intend to do harm. It's just an animal."

"Unfortunately it's a lethal and virulent animal, and one that may not be native to the region," Eckhart replied with a sorry look "Unlike, say, the *seelkee* of the Lower Fraser Salish or indeed the *selkie* of your Celtic ancestors, Jaime, there's no record of anything like this in the local mythology. Only since we Europeans began to move further into their lands."

"Well, I wish you all the best if you try to cull those crawlers," Cary grunted. "Don't come asking for my help."

"If we're lucky, it's just a matter of scooping them out and letting them dry."

"If we're really lucky, they can't take the cold," said Strike.

Jaime's arm had ceased to ache so acutely, and they happily accepted the invitation to stay for dinner. Eckhart—Norton to his friends, among whom they were now numbered—paid a messenger to fetch them a boxed dinner from a local tavern. Emory Strike's unusual complexion drew more attention from the public than he enjoyed, though after the first hour Jaime had largely forgotten about his piebald face. The private parts of Norton and Emory's home showed the touch of two bachelors of enterprising nature, blueprints and maps pinned to the walls, the bookshelves and cabinets brimming with not only books but curiously shaped rocks and small pieces of machinery, the carpet in the hallway flattened to a hue of murky brown that suggested a complete ignorance of all housekeeping. The dining room was in better nick, the pictures framed, the cabinet holding glassware and plates and not a chemist's retort as in the kitchen.

"I can hardly believe I'm opening the topic," Jaime said when they had done with their mock turtle soup and roast beef and the others were nursing rye-whiskeys. "but I must ask how it is you came to have that specimen in the first place. You're neither of you biologists."

"I am, in a sense," Norton replied. "If you consider a paleontologist to be a student of ancient biology. And my fate seems bound up with that animal. It's the reason we met." He smiled at Emory, who returned his gaze.

"Not true," he said, swirling the liquor in its heavy-bottomed glass. "We met because I asked you to feel me up."

"Ah. So you did. I assure you both, it was all on the up and up," he said as Cary looked at the ceiling and Jaime's face got very hot. "He was about to perform a magic trick, and asked me to prove the absence of trick wires or other flim flam."

"And?" Jaime asked, mainly to propel the conversation onward.

"Turns out he was entirely genuine," Norton said, a fondness growing on his face. "Though at first he despised me."

"You credit yourself," Emory replied evenly, though his eyes glittered in the homey light of the fire and tallow. "Really I didn't give you the least thought once you'd stopped pestering me."

"Is that so? I recall you saying something entirely different in that alleyway."

"That was after I'd realized my mistake."

"I'm so glad you did."

Cary cleared his throat, then nodded discretely towards the door. It was time to leave the couple to their intimate reminiscences, find somewhere quiet to sleep. Anywhere really, Jaime's eyelids drooping, the room closing around him. He bit his lip, shaking his head to clear it. Cary's voice was a submerged burbling as he spoke to the others.

"So where will you go?" Norton asked him.

"Wherever he goes," Cary said, jerking his thumb at Jaime. "Doesn't matter where. I'll be going with him."

"Do you mean it?" he asked, his voice ringing in his own ears as if he was deep underwater.

"Someone's got to mind you, don't they?" Cary said, his beard twitching as he pretended not to smile.

"Good luck," Jaime said, making no such attempt, glad to have reason to smile. "I haven't made it easy on you."

"Then I'll have to try harder, won't I?"

Buoyed by good feeling, Jaime pushed back from the table and stood. Sat again, grabbing at his arm as a searing pain shot through it. "I'm fine," he said through his teeth as the others sprang to their feet. "I just need some air."

Cary lent his arm for support but didn't argue with him. Leaving the dining room, the stench of the rotting specimen invaded his nostrils, and he clapped his hand over his mouth to keep from further soiling the carpet.

"You are not bloody well all right," Cary said as Jaime fell against the wall.

"Never been so tired in my life..."

"Good thing you've got me to take care of you."

"I'm lucky to have you, my friend."

"You got that right. Come on, let's find you somewhere to lie down."

He didn't have strength to argue. But he didn't need to be strong. Not all the time, not with Cary by his side. Cary, who had strength enough for two, and bravery to spare, and kindness. So much goodness in him, and Jaime wanted to tell him, name every way the world was better because of Cary Robb.

"Don't worry, I've got you," Cary said, and he lifted Jaime in his arms. Held him close. Together, they were strong. Together, they would survive. A warmth was spreading through him, not the hot stab of Rotherhithe's touch but a softening, a sweetness, not being poured into him but welling up from within, his body understanding before his mind could realize that this was how it felt to be loved.

Read on to learn more about *The Jaime Skye Chronicles*
(including the free novella *The Marvelous Mr. Strike*)

THE JAIME SKYE CHRONICLES

⊷ ∞ ⊶

BOOK 0: THE UNTOUCHABLE SKY

It's hard to stay ordinary when you have the power to reshape the world...
After a lifetime of cruel treatment for his illness, his strangeness, his
sensitivities, all Jaime wants is to be ordinary. Unfortunately he's heir
to a magical legacy with the power to reshape the world. Or so says the
most extraordinary man he's ever met.

A member of the Royal Society of Magisters, Lord Adrian Lear is
charming, persistent, and thoroughly convinced that Jaime is a wa-
ter-worker, able to bend the element to his will, to use as a tool or
weapon. A fact too strange for Jaime to believe, yet when their lives
are put in danger by Lear's age-old enemy, Jaime's untested power may
be the only hope they have to survive.

BOOK 2: SKYE'S RISING

Where the earth ends, the sky will rise

Born with a power he barely comprehends, Jaime Skye has struggled to find acceptance in the ordinary world. Yet every time he encounters the world of magic he's been told is his destiny, it seems to want him dead.

After vengeful mage brands him with a wasting spell, he and his companion Cary find themselves racing against time to uncover the cure. But a Waterman can only be healed by the waters of his birth, and it will take all his and Cary's strength and ingenuity to bring him home.

A home he's never known: the Isle of Angels.

What he finds there will challenge him in body and soul. For the Isle's guardian—his grandmother—is nothing like he imagined. And the true test of his powers is just beginning, as the enemy he knows only by name enacts a catastrophic plan to change the course of history.

SCAN THE CODE TO JOIN MY READERS CLUB AND BE THE FIRST TO READ

THE MARVELOUS MR. STRIKE

A TALE OF ELSEWHEN

A passionate story of first impressions and second chances from the world of The Jaime Skye Chronicles.

Norton Eckhart, PhD, is not afraid of miracles. Every fossil he finds is a tiny miracle, a symbol of science's triumph over the superstitions of a less enlightened age. He won't be swayed by charlatans and side-show fakers. Even if they are exceedingly handsome.

More than handsome, Emory Strike is magnetic, capturing Norton's imagination from the first moment he sees the man with the unusually coloured skin. Strike claims he is electric, with the power to control nature's most elusive—and deadly—phenomenon.

When Strike displays a power beyond Norton's rational understanding, can the man of science trust in the evidence of his senses? Or will his cold and lonely presumptions stand between him and the most fascinating man he's ever met?

ONE

To an ordinary eye it was a stone, but to Norton it was a minor miracle. A treasure house of secrets, a link to the distant past, to the very brink of Creation perhaps. New fossils, wholly new creatures were being found almost daily, to judge from the flurry of journals and *essais* and articles flying back and forth between the world's palaeontologists.

This was merely a cast of a trilobite, but whole and well preserved, an excellent specimen for use in class. The afternoon was drawing to an end, long rays of golden light gilding the fronts of the specimen cases and glaring in his eyes whenever he looked up from the work table. Blinking, his head throbbing faintly from the light and from almost certainly having forgotten to eat since his breakfast of coffee and zwieback, he returned the half-cleaned specimen to its drawer until tomorrow.

The corridor was gloomy after the sunlit study hall and he nearly walked into Miss Bramble. A high spirited bluestocking with far-reaching family connections, she had talked her way into the Natural History department of Trinity on the promise that she would not demand to be awarded a degree. She audited many a class and spent the rest of her time in the library, in between campaigning to be included on an expedition.

Though her mind was unparalleled, her intelligence seemed to have come at the cost of most feminine wiles and daintiness, her blouse fronts habitually spotted with soup and ink like any academic, pins forever falling from her dark hair, which became Medusan on a gusty day. From the number of books she consumed in a given month Eckhart was sure she never slept, and he often went out of his way to escort her to dinner in the faculty lounge, to be sure she was eating. And himself, for this was not the first day he'd lost to his work.

"Eck! Leaving so soon?" she asked as he picked up the pencil she'd dropped.

"It is nearly seven, Aurora."

"So it is. Are you going to dinner at the Captain's?"

Captain Pendleton was head of the geology department. An avid member of several literary societies, the fellow was desperate to encourage what little intellectual culture could be found in a city of fifteen thousand souls. For the last three or four weeks Norton had dined at the Captain's house on Thursdays, making excruciating small talk with the daughters of furriers and factory owners and trying to keep his progressive opinions on the Native Problem from starting a fight with the sons. Last week the Captain's likely son-in-law Henderson had been particularly combative, and Norton had resolved to avoid the cohort if he could.

"Not this week. I have another engagement," he said to Aurora as she accompanied him to the office he shared with the other junior professor Redding. He was showing too much eagerness, for her eyes lit up.

"Norton Eckhart, do you have a sweetheart?" Her smile softened at his horrified expression. "Don't look so scandalized, Eck. Men do have sweethearts."

"Naturally. Not me, though. Not that I wouldn't. Have one, I mean. It's only that I'm so busy. I would make a terrible lover. Beau, I mean..."

"I'll see you tomorrow, Eck." She left him at his door, which took him three tries to unlock with how badly his hands were shaking. The last thing he needed was to alienate one of his only friends with the truth of why he found those industrial daughters so tiresome. Or with his plans for the evening. There was something unavoidably shameful in a grown man with no children or girl-friend going alone to a carnival.

They had been setting up in a field west of the Humber River for the last two days, the flagpoles visible from the back of Trinity. The leaflets were plastered on every signboard and post between here and the Don. Twice they'd driven a wagon through the town to drum up attendees, and Norton had kept his head down when he heard them pass the college. Despite being a man of five-and-thirty and a doctor of natural science, Norton loved carnivals. They had been one of the few joys he'd known growing up. One of the few places Father chose not to accompany him, for the sour old Calvinist had objected to all such decadence.

His step light, he soon reached his boarding house, an older stone building which had been used as a hospital during the American invasion. The proprietress Mrs Selkie was in the dining room, setting out a cold supper for some of the older residents, and after greeting her as he liked to he hurried up to his room. There he washed his face and neck and powdered strategic parts of himself against the day's perspiration, then changed into the most frivolous garment he owned, a fine waistcoat of cream silk with little sprigs of lavender embroidered around the collar and edges. He hadn't stopped to think on seeing the uncut panels at a haberdasher's in Albany where he'd stopped to have a lost button replaced. He'd simply bought the thing, staying in town an extra two days for the tailor to make it up. An extravagance, he had worn it at most half a dozen times, for it was a bold garment for Toronto's staid tastes.

He considered a meal at a tavern, but for reasons he couldn't name his stomach was agitated, as if he was going to something more exciting than a dog and pony show. Crossing the bridge, he fell in with the scattered train of people heading for the carnival: families with children clustering about the mother's skirts or chasing each other through the crowd, swaggering groups of young men and sailors eager to lose their wages on midway games.

Several light gigs such as farmers use were parked together to the south of the fairground, which was dominated by a large striped marquee with a double-peaked roof where the main show undoubtedly took place. Several smaller tents and awnings stood to the north of this, the whole affair girded by a low fence of a single rope looped around short stakes. Norton paid his two bits at the gaudily painted ticket booth and entered the grounds on the heels of several students from his own department.

"Here to try your luck, Doctor?" Fitzwilliam said on spying him, his vividly striped waistcoat of green and blue making Norton feel like a pigeon among peacocks.

"Luck may be your only hope, young fellow," Norton replied, mollified by Fitzwilliam's flinch of embarrassment for being so forward with his elder. "You do understand many of these games are unwinnable by design, don't you?"

"Our pal Douglass is a crack shot with a cork-gun, Doctor Eck," said a fellow whose frothy sideburns Norton remembered from a first year class but not his name. "He's been practicing at home on tins of beans."

"Practice or no," Norton said to them generally, "if they've glued the bottles to the shelf, no mere cork will knock them down." He ought to speak more quietly, after that incident in Ohio where he'd gravely offended the carny and had to quit the fair in a hurry when the man had come after him with a cudgel. He left the youngsters to their evening and carried on to the sideshow.

Father had hoped he would go into medicine, but Norton detested the sight of blood. Innards were worse. Even fresh sausages could put him in an uneasy mood. Yet the peculiarities of the human form as displayed in a carnival freak-show held a sickening fascination he was unable to shake. The same unpleasant feeling gripping his stomach as earlier, he hesitated at the entrance to the tent, then stepped aside. These were ordinary people, no matter their afflictions. What he wished more than anything was to talk to them, discover how they navigated the world given the irregular vessels God had granted them. He couldn't stand being just another face in the pop-eyed crowd shuffling past, staring at them as if through glass, though certainly they would hear every word said about them, every shriek or laugh or mutter about their grotesquery. Feeling both high-minded and ashamed of his squeamishness, he carried on to the next tent.

TWO

The banner over the entrance to the green and pink striped tent read *Professor Ignatio's Wonders of the Ancient World.* Norton's catnip, for most of the self-declared wonders he had seen in similar venues had been fakes, recent corpses treated to appear like the embalmed remains of Egyptian kings, or cow bones freshly bought from the knackers, stained with tea or ash then labelled those of a dino-saur, that Englishman Owen's coinage for the massive beasts whose remains were turning up all over the American continent.

Ignatio's 'wonders' were stock in trade. The bones were larger than usual, suggesting they were from a draft horse rather than a cow. Several fine samples of petrified wood followed, arranged in front of a hinged mirror so one could view them from all sides. Then a narrow casket covered in peculiar markings, from which Norton averted his eyes as it made his stomach feel even worse. The last item on display was evidently the biggest draw, for it was attended by a swell-chested barker in a creased muslin suit and straw hat who one presumed was Professor Ignatio himself.

"Don't hesitate, my good man, to get your fill of Pandora's egg!" he said to Norton for the benefit of all hearers as he gestured grandly at the item on the plinth beside him. "Who knows when it might unleash the ancient horrors within?"

"So naturally you keep it on display at a public event?" Norton said mildly as he inspected the object, which looked nothing like an egg. More like a seed-case, its spiny carapace split into three distinct segments. It looked both wholly false and impossibly real, the crenulations and curves of its greasy brown surface too complex to be the product of design. "How did you come by this?" he asked.

"Very glad you asked, my friend," the carny said, tucking his thumbs in his armpits as he warmed to the topic. "This rarest of rarities washed ashore in the land of the fearsome Iroquois."

"You mean the Haudenosee? I've always found them very personable. And you say you stole this from them?"

The man's mouth snapped closed, his nostrils flaring. "I assure you, sir, this artefact came to me lawfully."

"Hmm. Artefact. Have you ever visited a museum of natural history?"

"Is that where you're from?"

"No, I'm from the university."

"Well, bully for you. Sir, I say, sir," he called to someone behind Norton, "Have you ever seen a genuine dinosaur's egg?"

Dismissed, Norton wandered out of the tent and on to the next, proclaimed by the placard beside it as *Mistress Vanora's House of Palmistry*. The small structure was painted dark blue and decorated with stars and crescent moons, the edges of the tent flaps painted with a border that jumbled together all manner of astrological and qabbalistic symbols. Very pretty and absolute gibberish, but after fossils there was little Norton enjoyed more than picking apart the tangle of feints and obfuscation behind a magic trick.

Inside she had all the usual trappings: dense, cloying incense and low lights, bright scarves and bits of tinsel pinned to the tent walls. The putative fortune teller fit the mold, being tiny, wrinkled, and brown, with long, ring-covered fingers and a great deal of kohl around her eyes. She sat behind a small table draped in a blue satin cloth with many snags and puckers.

"You will pay now," she said, extending a coin box affixed to a short stick, such as a tout might carry around a crowd.

"Shouldn't it be payment for services rendered?" he said, already warming to the challenge.

"You must pay first," she answered, waggling the box. "In case you don't like what I tell you."

Adequately logical, and so he dropped his pennies into the box which rattled emptily as she withdrew it. "It must have been a struggle," she said in the same lugubrious tone as he took the seat across from her. "Growing up with no brothers or sisters."

"I had a perfectly fine upbringing." A lucky guess, for he hardly wore his siblings' deaths written on his forehead.

"Your hand, sir." Watching her face, he laid his hand on the table, palm up. After a momentary inspection, she picked up the little brass censer and passed it over his palm, tracing the shape of a star. "Hm. Yes," she purred as she cradled his broad hand. "A very good upbringing. A very bad end."

"What a surprise," he said dryly. Not a single fortune teller had predicted anything other than a grisly death, though none had ever suggested the same means. "What will it be this time, trampled by elk or poisoned by tinned ham? Maybe struck by a runaway hand-truck as I'm crossing a railway?"

"It is not assured," she muttered, staring fixedly at his hand.

"Is anything?"

"That you will face terrible danger?" she said, raising her shadowed eyes. "Yes. That is very much assured. If you will survive it, that I cannot see."

"You needn't bother trying to frighten me," he said, but when he made to take his hand back she gripped it tightly, her narrow fingers encircling his wrist in a way that kept his palm open.

"You will be afraid enough in time. Here," and she stabbed her finger into his palm. "The trouble is here. The break in your heart line. Someone has hurt you. Or will very soon."

"Let me go," he said, trying to jerk his hand away, but her grip was like iron. Her face had changed, taking on a stilted, masklike appearance in the wavering candlelight.

"Soon..." she said in a hollow voice that seemed to echo in his skull. "Soon everything will change. You will not be the same man tomorrow that you are now."

"Heraclitus argued–"

She hissed at him, a strange silvery cast to her eyes. "Stupid mortal man. I tell you, you must change or he will die."

With a last desperate effort he yanked his hand from the fortune teller's savage grip, nearly tumbling backwards off the stool. It broke whatever spell had come over the woman, who slumped in her chair like a puppet whose strings had been cut.

Without waiting for her to rouse, Norton staggered out of the tent, recoiling from the assault of light and noise that was the carnival. The lanterns hung along the guy lines of the grand tent blazed like too-near stars, the raucous laughter of a passing group of people pummeling his ears. More fool him for skipping supper, and mopping his sweat-dampened face, he followed the general flow of people through the clamorous midway to where a crowd had gathered at the edge of the fairgrounds.

Another temporary fence of stakes and rope marked out an uneven circle. Shaded lanterns cast a bright glow towards the centre, and in the centre of the circle was a man.

THREE

He wanted to be seen. Why else be dressed in a suit of such a vivid yellow, one with the glow of the sunset along the horizon? He might have been wearing the least remarkable clothes and still be unmissable, with that bold slash of pale skin arching raggedly across the upper left of his handsome flint-brown face. A banner hung between two poles declared him to be *The Marvelous Mr. Strike, Master of Electricity.*

"Step up, step up, but no nearer than the barrier as marked, ladies and gents, boys and girls, viewers of all stripes and dispositions," Strike declared in a ringmaster's booming voice as Norton joined the crowd gathering along the barricade of rope. "For you are about to witness something you have never seen before nor are likely to ever see again. I ask those whom their doctor has cautioned against exertions of the heart to think twice before observing this phenomenon, ladies and gentlemen, viewers of all dispositions, for I would hate to be the agent of your untimely demise from shock."

A humorous titter passed through the crowd. Norton had heard much the same from other carnies, stimulating the audience into such a state of heightened expectation that any climax was a thrill. A cheap deal table stood near the man, holding an assortment of objects: a long goose feather, a handful of shiny coins, and a kerosene lantern. Further out in the circle, a small gang of bearded farmworkers armed with pitchforks was building what looked like a hayrick.

"As in any demonstration of the unbelievable," Strike went on, gesturing to the table. "I would ask that a member of the audience, a person I've never before met, assist me by inspecting these goods to prove there are no hidden threads or wires, and that this phenomenon is a product of the mysterious powers granted me by the miracle of God's grace. I assure you, no mechanical means shall be employed in these demonstrations."

He singled out two older children, a boy in a snug-fitting sailor suit and a girl with pink ribbons in her ringlets, to come up and handle each of the items in turn. "Do you believe these items free of interference?" he asked them when they had done.

"Yes, I undoubtedly do," declared the boy in a stagey bellow, puffing out his chest.

"Very good, young sir. And you, miss?" Casting an uncomfortable glance at the boy who stood rigidly at attention, she nodded, the ringlets bouncing. Strike then asked her to hold the feather, laying across her open hand.

"You may feel a slight enervation, miss, as I conduct this demonstration. Do not be alarmed." Gazing at the feather, he stepped back several paces, took a deep breath and released it. The girl squeaked a little cry as the feather stirred on her hand, not toppling to the side but slowly lifting until it stood upright on its quill.

"Young sir," said Strike without dropping his gaze from the feather, which had begun to rotate on the girl's trembling palm. "I would ask you to pass your hand above and below the feather to show that nothing is attached to it and that this is solely the levitational powers of electricity." His eyes enormous, his steps halting, the boy did as instructed, his flapping arm having no effect on the movement of the feather, which continued to rotate gently.

"There's nothing there," the girl said to him impatiently. Perhaps they were cousins, for the boy stuck out his tongue at her, earning a chuckle from the crowd.

"Indeed, my friends, there is no tangible thing connecting this feather to me" Strike said. "And yet..." He made a yanking motion and the feather leapt off the girl's hand and flew to his as if propelled from a gun. Another murmur passed through the crowd along with a smattering of applause as Strike thanked the children and sent them back to their parents.

"And now, I seek a young man of strong mind and disposition who would like to earn this coin." He held up a silver coin, waggling it to catch the ruby light. There was some scuffling among the crowd then one of the students threw up his hand. Strike waved him forward.

"Your challenge," he said as the youth inspected the coin, "is to remove that coin from my hand. Do so and it's yours." He took it back and placed it on the palm of his hand. "At your leisure, good sir."

Glancing at his friends, the young man snickered, then reached out to pluck the coin from Strike's open hand. Instead his fingers slid over it like it wasn't there. His smug grin falling away, he tried again, closing his fingers around the edge of the coin but failing to move it. Red-faced, he looked at his own hand, then at the coin. "It's glued to your hand," he declared.

"I assure you it is not," said Strike, picking up the coin with ease. "You may inspect my hand as well."

The other man grabbed it roughly, running his fingers over Strike's palm. "Then you glued the coin."

"Again, you may assure yourself this is not the case," Strike replied cheerfully as he gave him the coin again.

"Let me try," said one of his friends.

"How hard can it be?" said another.

"That coin is a plug."

"Let's split the difference, friend," Strike said as the crowd began to shuffle its feet. "You did in fact remove the coin, through the power of scientific inquiry. It's yours to keep."

A small cheer went up from the man's friends as Strike steered him back towards them. "And now for a more vigorous display of my abilities, may I ask a man of science to assist me?" he said, returning to the centre of the ring.

"Where's Doctor Eck?" A chorus rose from the Trinity students. It was echoed by others around Norton, who found himself being shoved towards the front of the crowd.

FOUR

The sun had dropped below the horizon, little peach-hued clouds dotting the violet sky, the man named Strike blazing like a miniature sun as he beckoned to Norton. Transfixed by the sight, he nearly went sprawling over the rope fence, earning a few titters, some unkinder laughs. Strike made nothing of it as he ushered Norton towards the table.

"And what is your profession, sir?" he asked.

"Professor. Of natural History. At Trinity. The university."

"Then you're just the man I wanted." As Strike smiled, a silent hopeless feeling ignited in Norton's chest, echoing in his loins. A feeling he usually tried to negate or ignore. Where friends were hard to find, lovers were inconceivable, and he wasn't needful nor brave enough to seek relief in the back alleys round the dockyard, nor in the molly house said to be operating on the Scarborough bluffs. Strike was magnetic, in the poetical sense, drawing Norton to him by his mere existence.

"Can you assure the audience that there are no fuses or sulfur or other combustibles to alter the function of this lantern?" Strike asked.

With some difficulty he turned his attention to the kerosene lamp on the table, which was to all appearances a very ordinary lamp. "None whatsoever."

"Thank you. Please step back several paces. Don't run off yet, though," he added as Norton made to return to the audience. "I'll have need of you again."

The feeling in Norton intensified, like someone had turned up his wick. The other man's words meant nothing, the implications solely in Norton's lonesome mind. He retreated as did Strike, the lantern on the table between them. Gazing at the lantern with intense focus, Strike held out his hand, palm down, then snapped his fingers. White light sparked between his fingertips, a corresponding spark flaring at the base of the lamp wick, which ignited handily. An approving murmur rose along with another burst of applause.

"And now a final demonstration," Strike said as he stripped off his sunny yellow jacket. He passed it to a carnival worker in an acrobat's blouse and tight hose, then began to unbutton his waistcoat as a tittering whisper passed through the audience.

"No, this is not in service of any prurient interest," Strike said as he shrugged out of his braces and started on his violet cravat. "But to prove conclusively that my talents lie solely within me and not in any incendiary devices I have hidden on my person. You will further note that I have had nothing to do with the placement of this here hay," he went on, gesturing to the hayrick behind him.

One might have lead a herd of elephants past Norton and he would have seen nothing but the shape of Strike's bare shoulders as they emerged from his shirt. The skin condition which had touched Strike's face continued across the rest of his body, mottled patches of fair skin banding his arms, a streak extending down the nape of his neck from beneath his dark, closely cut hair.

"These fine men are from your locality and will attest I've laid no incendiary material in this hay," Strike said, indicating the farm men standing by their dray with matched frowns. "Furthermore, they will remain at attention, so that the fire does not become a danger to you or your fine metropolis. I would now ask the man of science to inspect me to prove there are no wires or fuses connecting me to this incendiary material."

He advanced on Norton and stopped, his arms outstretched. Norton was meant to touch him. To run his hands over the man's half-bare body in search of wires or lucifers, he guessed. He'd have to go on guesses for speech was beyond him.

From his vantage behind the table, Norton could see the faces of the audience, a panoply of shock, delight, disgust, awe, and confusion. Propelled by a lifetime of surrendering to public expectation, Norton bit down on his tongue and performed the task with brusque efficiency, taking care to avoid the man's rosy nipples, the soft indent of his navel, which existed in its own little patch of sweetly pink skin. Thank God for the dark, for loose trousers, for being less interesting than someone else, and he shuffled backwards into the shadows as Strike faced the audience once more.

"One more point I must make absolutely clear to one and all," he said in a firm tone with no echo of showmanship. "Please, I implore you, for your safety and the safety of others, do not attempt what I am about to do. This demonstration relies upon properties of electricity known only to myself and a few rare practitioners of this science. In ordinary settings, electricity is a deadly force, the power of Prometheus and the wrath of Olympus in one. It kills without mercy, and mortal strength alone cannot defeat it."

"Again, please do not try this at home. What you are about to witness should not in fact be possible. The means of it are beyond articulating, which is a scientific way of saying such talents as mine retain an element of mystery even to myself."

"Then how do you know it's working?" Fitzwilliam called from near the edge of the crowd.

"May the results speak for themselves," Strike replied, smiling hugely. He snapped his fingers and a white-hot burst flared from his fingertips. An interested murmur passed through the crowd and Strike turned to the hayrick. As he gazed at it, a strange luminosity passed over his face, seen only by Norton. Strike's eyes rolled back to the whites as he raised his right hand overhead, hand open as if to catch something. He took a great breath then threw his hand towards the hayrick, which burst into flames as a searing bolt of lightning erupted from within it and went streaking towards the sky.

The crack of thunder followed instantaneously, causing several in the crowd to cry out, others to throw their hands over their ears. A small child began to wail. The farmers sprang to douse the flames with shovelfuls of soil. As the acrobat and girl in a blouse and Turkish trousers worked their way through the crowd, Strike winked at Norton then turned and bowed deeply. The applause was scattered and not much louder than the clink of coins into a box.

FIVE

As the crowd dispersed, Strike gathered up his trick coins and feathers in a bit of canvas. The rigid focus had faded from his expression as swiftly as it came, his smile flashing in the glow of the lantern as Norton approached.

"May I say, that was truly an exciting piece of showmanship."

"We like to give the people their money's worth," Strike replied, the flickering light gilding his bare arms and deepening the shadows of his collar bones and Norton was staring and needed to speak or else walk away.

"You handled the crowd magnificently," he said, his tongue tripping on the last word. "Though I wonder if anyone has ever caused you trouble."

"About the coin, you mean?" Strike said. "There's always a few who feel bidden to prove themselves. But we look after our own. They wouldn't get off the fairground without answering for any trouble, as you say." He passed the lantern to the girl in the trousers then gripped the edge of the table. "Couldn't give a fellow a hand carrying this, could you?"

"Of course!" Norton lifted the other edge of the flimsy table and they carried it across the bent grass to a plain canvas tent in a row of similar set behind the midway, where the acrobat was waiting with Strike's shirt and jacket.

"Thanks, Lou," Strike said. "And to you, Dr Eck. You seem to be someone of esteem in these parts."

"Oh. That's their pet name for me. Really it's Eckhart. Norton Eckhart. At your service." They shook hands at last (o joy!) the press of the man's hot skin sending a shiver of unwanted pleasure up Norton's arm.

"What's your field?" Strike asked as he pulled on his shirt, apparently unselfconscious of letting a strange man watch him dress, which was somehow as confronting as having watched him disrobe.

"Paleontology," Norton replied, his voice cracking like one of his student's. "Old bones, for the lay person," he added as Strike frowned.

His expression brightened at once. "You're a dinosaur hunter?"

"In so many words. Though my specialty is crinoids. A long-extinct sea creature, though to the eye their fossils often resemble plants."

"Do you know much about electricity?"

"I'm aware of the popular literature, though it's quite out of my bailiwick. It seems a fascinating phenomenon."

"It certainly is," Strike replied with another flash of that showman's smile. "I'd be curious to see what your Trinity men are doing with it."

"Come tomorrow and I'll get you a meeting with the dean of physical sciences," Norton said without the faintest idea how he might do so, given he was a junior adjunct of no distinction in an entirely separate school of the college.

"Don't trouble yourself," Strike thankfully said. "I'm more inclined to poking around a lab and talking to researchers."

"Then that's what we'll do. I'm sure it won't be a problem."

"You have much sway in the other departments?"

"Er, no, but, well, I'll try. For you. Because you clearly know a lot and maybe they'd want to meet you as well. Really, I feel you're wasted in such a setting as this." He indicated the tents, the table. "You should be applying your knowledge with more purpose."

"I've plenty of purpose, if you please," Strike replied, his broad chest swelling proudly. "The last thing I need is the approval of a bunch of stuffy old men who can't trust what they see with their eyes except when it comes to the color of my skin. Thank you but I'll stick with making my own name and making a buck while I'm at it."

"Certainly you don't fit the mold of what the college expects, but that's due to change. And is not the very foundation of scientific inquiry to doubt one's first impression?"

He snorted, looking at Norton with a hard expression. "Every college man I've met has been well convinced of his first impression. That I'm a charlatan or fraudster, mainly."

"Well...would they be wrong?" As Strike hissed a breath through his teeth Norton realized his misstep. "Er, that is, I do understand your need to make a living but doesn't it wear at you?"

"I'm not sure I understand your meaning," Strike said with an acid tension.

"You mustn't worry that I'll reveal any of your means. On that you have my word. But really, Mr. Strike, just because we watched men make that haystack doesn't mean you didn't, well, bury dynamite there this morning."

"You're more than welcome to look for evidence of that, Mr. Eckhart," Strike replied, gesturing curtly to the blackened mass of hay.

"Dr. Eckhart, if you please," Norton murmured by rote, for it had taken some months of gentle persistence to remind Father that he'd received his doctorate. Yet in the moment it was another misstep as Strike spat to one side.

"I don't please. In fact, I don't like your manner at all, Eckhart."

"I swear, I won't tell a soul."

"You saw all there is to tell. If you don't believe me, that's your problem." He snapped his fingers and white hot light burst in an arc between his fingertips, dazzling Norton's eyes.

"Mr. Strike, I apologize," Norton said, the bag of coins rattling as Strike scooped it off the table. "I didn't mean to offend you."

"What did you think would happen when you called me a liar and a faker?"

"I didn't say you were either of those things!" Norton pleaded. Strike had turned to enter the tent and whirled to face him.

"But you meant it, didn't you? You don't believe what you saw. You think I'm lying to you even now, don't you?"

"No! Not lying, as such."

"Then what?" Strike hissed, looming closer. "Am I delusional? Or is it possible you can't imagine anything exists outside your tidy world of lists and labels, your shelves full of dead things. This world is bigger than you know, Eckhart," he said, prodding him in the chest with a stiff finger. "One day you're going to be in for a nasty surprise."

Norton had just time to feel his heart fall to pieces when the night entire was rent by a horrific explosion. Figures burst from the tents around them, carnival crew and performers in various states of undress, as smoke began to billow from behind the big tent, lit a lurid orange by the flames.

"What should I do?" Norton said as people started running towards the fire.

Strike rounded on him, his face surreal in the flickering light. "Go to the devil, for all I care."

SIX

He'd done everything wrong. Ruined any chance of gaining Strike's friendship, even his tolerance. Once again he'd been the architect of his own failure, spouting reckless opinions to the one person whose favor he wished to obtain. Though he feared the midway would be a melee, most patrons had already left, only a few huddled groups hastening past the empty stalls for every carnival hand had been called to the fire.

Passing the fortune teller, he paused at the sound of shouting coming from Professor Ignatio's tent which was shaking as if in a vicious wind. There was a loud bang and pained grunt, then a swarm of men in dark clothes came out of the tent, struggling to carry a large and bulky object swathed in canvas. One spied him and grunted to his fellows and they legged off into the gloom.

Barely breathing, Norton pushed open the tent flap. The dinosaur egg's plinth was bare, the shiny cloth fallen to the dirt. The showman Ignatio lay there as well, a dark wetness spreading from beneath his crumpled form.

Blood. From a wound, Ignatio groaning and clutching his shoulder as he rolled to his back.

"I shall summon help!" Norton cried as his stomach attempted to climb out through his throat.

"Never mind me," Ignatio rasped, attempting to sit upright. "If you wanna be a hero, retrieve my property!" As Norton dithered in the entrance of the tent, unable to tear his eyes from the hideous red stain spreading across the man's chest, a woman in a bright pink tutu pushed past him.

"Walter!" she shrieked, dashing to Ignatio and falling to her knees beside him.

"You've got help now, that's good, I'll go and find the egg," Norton blurted as he fumbled with the tent flap.

"And for the love of God, don't let it get wet!"

The fire had illuminated the field for some distance and he could see the thieves off in the field, struggling with their misshapen spoils. Yet even were he to catch them, he had no way to stop them, and he lurched about in a state of helpless frustration. People were running to and fro singly and in twos and threes, and when he saw Strike he leapt to intercept him.

"Get out of my way," Strike spat, trying to step around him.

"Listen to me, they've stolen Ignatio's egg."

Strike wheeled around and grabbed the shoulder of Norton's jacket. "Who stole it?"

"I don't know but they went that way." He gestured as best he could in the thieves' direction, for Strike's grip had half yanked him off his feet, so much that he nearly fell when Strike let him go and took off in pursuit.

Norton didn't like fear. Some men relished it, spent their days seeking it, or at least not minding if they felt it. Those were the men who scaled mountains, sailed oceans, fought wars and forged the future of humankind. Norton was not such a man. The monsters he confronted were so long dead they inspired only wonder, and a healthy respect for the wisdom of Creation that separated their kind from his in the span of Earth's history.

He disliked injustice more. The same wisdom that let the dinosaurs expire before humans arose had provided resources enough on Earth to care for everyone, yet some persisted in acting as if their gain depended on another's loss. Simple economics, though he'd had several economists tell him otherwise. Theft distorted the natural flow of capital and labour, whether done by oligarchs or monopolists or by plain old pick-pockets. That egg was someone's livelihood, and Norton was if nothing else a man who adhered to his principles.

All of which logic did nothing to comfort him as he took off in pursuit of the much fleeter Strike and an armed gang of unknown thieves in possession of what was essentially a large piece of wood. Neither did it stop him, and he nearly barreled into Strike who had stopped and was staring into the gloom.

"What are you doing here? You're going to get yourself killed," Strike said.

"Do you even know where they went?"

"I can find them." He clasped his hands together out in front of his chest and pulled like dragging a barge pole. A strange sucking sensation that made Eckhart's scalp prickle passed through the air, then Strike threw his hands forward and open, releasing the force he'd gathered. A blue-white star burst overhead far out across the field, lighting it like a stage, the knot of men easily seen struggling with their burden a quarter mile away.

Strike took off running again. Norton followed, though he was sweating, and his feet hurt, and he really didn't know what help he could be. But scampering back to the carnival leaving Strike to face the unknown alone seemed the acme of cowardice. What if the men had pistols or knives? Many people considered free in Canada were considered chattel south of the border, and this perhaps is what frightened Norton the most, what kept him on Strike's heels.

As the light above them faded, one of the men stepped apart from the others. Something flashed in front of him, but before Norton could connect the flare to the loud retort which followed Strike had tackled him to the ground. As Norton lay groaning Strike rolled off him and up to standing, then swept the air as he had before to send a dart of blue-white light lancing towards the other man. It struck not the man but the gun which exploded in his hand. He fell, shrieking and clutching his face.

"Was that necessary?" Norton said as Strike hauled him to his feet.

"He would have gladly killed us," Strike hissed. "He'll get no sympathy from me."

He dashed off again, but the fall had bruised Norton's side and he could only hobble in pursuit, suppressing his churning horror as he passed the man groaning in the matted grass, left by his co-conspirators to die. Strike's star had faded and the moon was a mere crescent on the horizon behind and his only guide in the dark was the grunting of the crew of armed men.

Strike's star...that bolt...and Norton had doubted him. Not trusted his eyes, not trusted the evidence, instead favoring his prejudiced view that any act playing at a carnival was by its nature corrupt. Deprived of sight by the deepening darkness, his mind supplied the face of the fortune teller, the silvery cast to her eyes as she crushed his hand in her fervent grip and foretold imminent death.

You must change or he will die...

SEVEN

Stumbling over the rutted ground, his breath rattling in his lungs, Norton chased Strike and the gang towards the river. Ignatio had said not to get the so-called dinosaur's egg wet, with the fervour of a man speaking his last words on earth, and Norton was inclined to believe him, no matter what lies the man might have told in his colourful career. There was something deeply alien about the object, the pocked and bubbled surface like a toad's back, its oily gleam under the lanterns. It was either valuable or dangerous. Or both.

As his eyes adjusted to the darkness, Norton could make out the forms of the trees ahead. Strike and the gang had disappeared into the thin band of woods and Norton paused, unsure where to enter. Pulling his jacket closed over his delicate waistcoat, he shouldered through a gap in the undergrowth and found himself in the middle of a bramble patch. Thorns clinging to his trousers and tearing at his hands, he made to retreat, and was about to whistle just to see if he'd get a reply when a chorus of shouts arose from his left.

"To the devil with your duke," Strike snarled above the others. "You'll not take me alive."

In the burst of light Eckhart saw him in silhouette. Saw as well the pair of thieves creeping up behind him, but even as Norton drew breath to shout a warning they leapt upon him. One of the men caught Strike's arms behind his back but let go with a howl of pain as Strike slammed his head into the brute's nose. Then four men closed on him and he fell.

"No!" He hadn't meant to cry out. Now they knew he was there. Ignoring the scrape of the thorns and the squelch of the mud soaking through his boots, Norton kicked his way free of the brambles.

"Who in the hell—" someone grunted.

"Never mind who," a man replied tersely in the cultured tones of a wealthy Briton. "He can regret his folly in the next life."

At another flash and a retort and Norton dropped to the ground, trading a faceful of wet mud and brambles for a gutful of lead. Of all the days to wear his finest clothes, but when he set out this evening he could hardly have predicted chasing armed thieves through the moonless woods.

"Find him," said the Englishman. "There are to be no witnesses."

As the long beams of their lanterns swept the forest Eckhart heard the shouts of carnival folk, but his limbs had turned to stone, his heartbeat so loud his teeth hurt. The light gleamed off the edges of the leaves in front of his nose.

"There he is!" The light grew and grew. Eckhart raised his head to see a pair of muddy boots.

"Get up before I kick your teeth in," said the owner of the boots. The loathing in the voice drove Eckhart to his feet as surely as the threat. He was denied a sight of his captor by the man opening the shutter of the lantern and shining it full on his face.

Once, when young and full of frontier spirit, Eckhart had gotten lost in the forest and come across a cougar stretched out on a sunny rock. The beast had watched his every trembling backwards step, the tip of its tail twitching like any cat's, its jowls stained with the blood of the deer it had been feeding on. Time slowed to the same icy trickle as the men bound Eckhart's hands roughly behind his back and began to drive him towards the river.

"Who is he?" the Englishman asked.

"No one!" he cried. "Really, I'm not."

"Then no one's going to mind when I slit your throat."

A visceral thrill shot through Norton's heart, his captors tightening their grip as he thrashed. "Please don't kill me!" he blurted, pressing his thighs together against the liquid terror gripping his bowls. "I know all sorts of things. How to get on with the natives, how to get around the country—"

The man hit him, an open-handed blow to the side of his head, frightening for its casualness. "You're an even bigger fool than you appear if you think we've any need of you."

"Where is it?" Norton gasped as the man turned away, if only to prolong the last moments of his life. "The professor's egg. What have you done with it?"

"Professor?" he drawled. "Don't tell me you believed that charlatan?"

"It doesn't matter what I believe. It's not yours to steal."

"Neither is it his."

"Where's Strike?" The man whirled about and struck him again. Harder, rattling Norbert's jaw.

"Shut him up," he said tersely to the men holding his arms. "We'll throw the body in the lake." He stomped away, branches snapping under his feet. How could the carnival folk not hear them?

"Ah well, let's get this over with." said the man to Norbert's left.

"I don't want to drag a body all that way," said the other man. "Let's do it on the boat."

Gripping him under the armpits, they steered him through the undergrowth to the bank of the river. They were only a mile from the mouth of the river and the far bank was lost in shadows. A flat-bottomed river boat lay close by the shore, lanterns hung at prow and stern. Strike sat near the middle, his hands tied like Norbert's, a sack over his bowed head. They were both going to die for nothing. For that fancily carved piece of wood wrapped in a filthy canvas that a pair of the conspirators were currently wrestling down the sloping riverbank.

"Go on, get down there," the man to his left said as Norbert balked at the top. "Don't cause any trouble and I'll try and make it quick."

"Whatever he's paying you, I'll double it," Norton babbled as they forced him down the slope. "No, triple it. My father's very well-off, he'll reward for saving me if you'd just–"

He was silenced by a coarse hand clamped around his throat. "It's too late for that," the man said. "You heard his lordship. No witnesses."

"But I've barely seen a th—"

The hand tightened. "For a clever man you're not very bright, are you?"

EIGHT

They left him on the barge, seated on a narrow slat amidships, his back to Strike, his ears ringing from their slaps and churlish laughter. On shore, the men grappled with the oddly shaped egg they had stolen from Ignatio. Another man stood at the top of the bank watching them struggle, possibly the Englishman, his rank evident from the gleam of his high boots, his smooth face a death's mask in the flickering light of the lantern at his feet.

"Eck?" Strike murmured.

"I'm here." He extended his fingers. Found Strike's.

"Sorry you got dragged into this," he said, pinching Norton's fingers between his.

"I couldn't let them take you."

Strike's fingers tensed, relaxed. "Where am I?"

"On a barge."

"And Ignatio's egg?"

"They're about to bring it aboard."

Strike's fingers tensed again. "What did he tell you about it?"

"Not a lot. He'd been shot—"

Strike hissed, his fingers clenching Norton's painfully. "They're going to pay for this," he whispered fiercely.

"Sit back a little and I might be able to reach your wrists." Strike wriggled closer. Hunching his shoulders to raise his hands, Norton began to feel about for the knot.

"Eck..." Strike murmured.

"Hmm..."

"What's your name?"

"Me? Norton. You?"

"Emory."

"Of course."

He chuckled softly. "What do you mean, of course? How would you know?"

"I didn't. It just feels right. It feels like it belongs to you."

The brutes had done their job well, the knot tucked underneath and near impossible to reach, and he managed only to tear his thumbnail and hurt his shoulders. He gave up as the men on shore began to bicker.

"Will you get on?" the Englishman snapped over the griping of the two men bearing the egg. "If you aren't aboard when the carnies catch up, you'll be joining that twit at the bottom of the lake."

"You might help us if you want it done quicker," one of the men said under his breath as they began to splash towards the barge. His friend gasped, shaking his head with a tiny frantic motion.

"Yes, what was that you said?" the man on shore asked, pushing back his heavy cloak to reveal the pistol in his belt, the scabbard at his hip.

"Nothing, your lordship," the thief blurted. His heel caught on a root in the churning silt and he fell backwards with the egg in his lap.

"You imbecile!" the Englishman shouted, stamping his polished boot. "You were told expressly not to get it wet."

"It's falling to pieces!" the thief cried, wrapping his arms around it as the lord started down the slope. The water had begun to seethe, foaming like the bubble of carbonate in acid. Suddenly he cried out, his body lurching.

"Snake!" he shrieked, trying to shove the egg away. "There's a snake in—" The snake must have bit him for he screamed. Not a cry of surprise but a shriek of purest terror, rising in panic as others splashed into the water to help him.

His partner was feeling about in the water in search of the egg. "There's another snake!" he cried, lurching upright. And then he fell, like someone had pulled his feet from under him, Norton catching sight of his astonished expression before he disappeared under the churning water.

"What's happening?" Strike hissed.

"It's come alive!"

"Ignatio's egg."

"I think it hatched. Oh God!" Strange fleshy tendrils were rising from the water, whipping about to grab men by the arm, the neck, and drag them shrieking under the surface, a sailor's nightmare come to hideous life. Norton's own nightmares, the water red with blood and roiling with foul intestinal tubes, the air rent with screams and desperate prayers.

"I need this rotten thing off me," Strike said, shaking his head violently in hope of dislodging the sack.

"Lean back," Norton said. One eye on the lethal scene in the water, he stood up cautiously on the rocking barge. Reaching behind, he found the corner of the coarse sack, which was thankfully not tied around Strike's neck and came off easily.

"Jesus!" he cried as he took in the hellish sight. "Damnation, Eck, what have we done?"

"We didn't do anything. It's him." He nodded to the Englishman pacing the bank.

"Rotherhithe!" Strike hissed as Norton sat again. "No surprises there."

"You know him?"

"Yes, and I wish I'd killed him when I had the chance." He began to fight in earnest against the rope binding his wrists.

"Are we safe on the boat?"

"Safer than them," he said grimly, nodding towards the frothing water, the screaming men.

"Did Ignatio know what he had?"

"No idea. Is he alive?"

"He was when I left him."

The twinkling lanterns and shouting voices of the carnival folk were converging on them. Teeth bared, Rotherhithe took a last look at the nightmare scene then scrambled up the bank and disappeared into the darkness.

"Damn that devil!" Strike cried, springing to his feet. "He's getting away."

A few of the thieves had made it ashore and lay gasping on the spit of gravel. One of the unlucky floated facedown amid the reeds. As they watched, a red tendril emerged from the murky water to wrap around the dead man's neck and pull him under the surface. Eyes fixed on the place where the body had been, Strike sat again, leaning against Norton. "Never mind."

But perhaps the monster had sated its appetite or had merely become aware of its freedom, for as the first beams of the search party's lanterns struck the water the creature gathered its lashing tentacles and shot away down the river, heading for the lake, the ripple of its passage soon lost in the ceaseless current.

NINE

They spoke to the police. They spoke to Mr. Bewdley, the owner of the carnival, a bustling, avuncular man with a booming voice and eyes that blinked too often. They spoke to Ignatio in his cluttered, smoke-tarred caravan, the woman in the pink tutu standing impatiently by the door with her arms crossed and toe tapping. The bullet had struck Ignatio in the shoulder and not the chest as Norton had feared, and he was sitting up in the bed that filled the end of his caravan, chewing on an unlit cigar, his arm and torso bandaged heavily.

"That's a darn shame you had to go through all that," he said, patting Strike's hand like he was the one bereaved. "But I suppose I'm better off without the cussed thing." His nurse grunted in agreement, and soon after shooed them out of the caravan.

"Can I go home yet?" Norton asked as they walked the unlit midway.

"I guess so," Strike replied, stifling a yawn. "I'll walk with you."

"Don't feel obliged."

"I'll feel better knowing you got home safely."

It seemed churlish to refuse, even though Strike was still wearing his wet and filthy yellow suit. Norton looked—and felt—equally squalid and so said nothing as they walked the short distance to the bridge.

"I must apologize," Strike said once they'd crossed the echoing bridge (at a faster pace than Norton usually kept.) "I surely didn't mean for you to involve yourself like that."

"I'm glad that I did," Norton replied. "And it's I who should apologize. I was wrong about you. I did think you were a charlatan. I did just what you said, let my academic mind blind me to real evidence. but I was wrong. You're not a faker. You're...you're a fossil."

"I'm an old rock?" Strike said with a puzzled grin.

"No. I mean that you're a miracle, hiding in plain sight." Norton felt in his pocket, relieved to find the hard shape of the fossil. "We found such a huge cache I chose not to record this little one," he said as he handed it to Strike "I take it with me everywhere."

Strike felt the underside of the smooth pebble and turned it over. "Oh...will you look at that?"

"Hiding in plain sight," Norton said as Strike rubbed his thumb over the perfectly cast fossil of a tiny crinoid.

"Thank you for what you did tonight," he said, passing it back to Norton. "You saved my life."

"You could have managed. You, the master of the marvelous."

He laughed dryly. "Maybe. But I don't want to have to..." He paused to take a deep breath, not meeting Norton's eye. "I once killed a man," he said with a quaver in his normally strong voice. "You should know that about me. He wanted me dead, nearly achieved it. I didn't know what I was doing, you see? Didn't know my own strength. I didn't know I had this cursed power."

"It woke in me that night," he went on in a hollow tone. "But I couldn't stay a slave. Not me. Son of a free man. That's how I ended up a houseboy and not in the field. Because I could read. And Hannity the foreman, he hated me for it, hated that a house boy was smarter than him. Dirt was smarter than him. If it hadn't been me it would have been somebody else who'd have done him in. If the devil didn't find him first." His steps faltered, his arms locked over his stomach.

"Are you hurt?" Norton asked stupidly.

"It's nothing," Strike grunted through his clenched teeth.

"I don't blame you for being frightened. I was terrified."

"It was like it was happening all over again," he blurted. "Like nothing I'd done in the years since had made a lick of difference. I was still just meat."

His heart torn in two, Norton gripped Strike's shaking shoulder, wanting to communicate his empathy, knowing that no words could match the man's suffering. The touch was enough, as Strike fell against him, shuddering as he burrowed his face into the curve of Norton's shoulder.

He gasped as a strange tingling began spreading down his chest. Trembling, he gripped the other man tighter, breathing into the luminescent pulse arising from the place where Strike's skin touched his. Strike sighed, softening against him, his arms winding around Norton's waist, until they embraced as intimately as any lovers, hidden from the world by nothing but the shadow between two wavering gas-lamps.

He ought to let go. Stop clutching this stranger to him, their bodies so close together he felt the rising of Emory's desire, a desire that matched his own. He ought to walk away, let this night fade into memory. Yet everything he'd done in life, every one of his achievements, was in opposition to what he ought to have done. He ought to be a doctor, a husband, a puppet of his father's will, a slave of a different sort. He had thrown aside every cozy advantage to pursue his heart's desire. He saw no reason to change.

Not now, as this marvelous man raised his head to look him in the face. He brushed his fingers over Norton's cheek, trailing a tingling path across his skin like his hands were full of stars.

"Damnation," Strike whispered. Then kissed him.

Electric, the first touch of Strike's mouth to his sending a bolt of sensation and longing shooting through him. Astonishing, Strike's unreal power flowing into him as his tongue trailed across his Norton's lips. Irresistible, surpassing his imagination, for if all kisses were thus, no one would ever stop kissing to do such trivial things as breathe. Shivery waves of sensation spread down his back and across his scalp as Strike threaded his strong hands into Norton's unkempt hair. He might have happily stood there until the end of time if not for the lonesome toll of a muted church bell ringing the hour.

"Don't leave me," he gasped when Strike lifted his head.

"I won't," he said, smoothing Norton's hair back from his burning face. "But this might be nicer to do indoors.

"You'll need to be quiet."

"I can do that."

His heart in his throat, his hand in Strike's, he led them to his rooming house, where they crept upstairs and slipped into his room without speaking a word. He'd never tested Mrs Selkie's knowledge of men's private lives and wished not to do so now. Yet he couldn't let this chance slip him by, surrender to common sense and bid this man good night. Whatever Strike wished of him, he would give, tonight even if never again.

TEN

B rave intentions, yet as they crept up the stairs to his room his nerve failed, as he thought of the overcrowded bookshelves, the dusty carpet, the litter of paper spilling from the desk. Had he even made his bed? Unlikely, as inviting someone to share it had been the farthest thing from his mind that morning. Not a thing about him was inviting, his clothes rank with mud, his manner unsophisticated.

He nearly asked if they might leave the room unlit, but no sooner had he closed the door then Strike was there close behind him, his sizzling hands easing Norton's jacket off his tense shoulders.

"I...I've never done this before," he blurted as Strike reached around to unbutton his dirty waistcoat.

"You've never brought someone here?" Strike asked, his hands pausing on Norton's chest.

"Or anywhere," he said, turning in the circle of his arms. "I don't want to disappoint you."

"I don't have much to compare to, if you want the truth."

"I do. I want to know everything about you."

"A sentiment you may come to regret," he said with a wry chuckle.

"I won't. I'm sure of it." With the same surety he'd felt when he'd rejected Father's offer of reading medicine at Harvard in favour of 'picking bones' for a living. The same sense of rightness as the day he found his first fossil without anyone's aid, when he'd seen the divine truth with his own eyes. Perhaps Emory Strike was not divine, but he was of God's making, and he was here now and it felt so very right. Norton was being gifted a miracle, and he would not let it go.

They kissed again, and this time when he felt Strike's tongue trace his lips he opened to him, a thrill of pleasure racing through him as Strike's tongue tasted his in small, sensuous licks. He tensed as Strike's firm hands slid down to his waist.

"Do you want to stop?" he asked.

"I don't know," Norton stammered. "No. I mean, no, please don't stop. I'm sorry."

He laughed again but kindly, trailing one sparking finger along Norton's jaw. "Let's get you out of these dirty clothes." Not dropping his gaze, Strike tugged loose the knot of Norton's cravat then slowly drew it from around his neck.

"And you?" Norton managed to ask as Strike dropped the cravat and started on his buttons again.

He smiled, a slow spreading of his lips that set of an echoing bloom of heat inside Norton. "As you like," he said, sliding his hands down Norton's back.

"I really don't know."

"What if we kiss again?"

"Yes, let's try that."

Kissing all the while, they undressed one another, eliminating any suspicion Norton held that their first kiss had been born of panic and not a deeper passion. Emory Strike was indeed a miracle, for everywhere his body bore signs of the hardship he'd endured. The scars did nothing to diminish his masculine beauty, nor did the patches of pale skin that barred his arms, his chest, his face.

Norton had left a little water in the ewer and they paused to wipe the clammy feel of the river water off their legs. And then they were nude, face to face in the calamity of Norton's room, and he didn't know what to do. It seemed impossible to have travelled so far in a single night when all he'd done was cross the river.

"I have a bed," he said foolishly after a stilted moment.

"That's...handy."

"We could go to it."

"We could," Strike replied, smiling as he took his hand and drew him nearer.

"I'm sorry to be so...I don't know." He gestured around, ample evidence of his shortcoming piled around them.

"It's okay, Norton. I didn't come here for your housekeeping."

A little thrill shot through him at the sound of his name on the other man's lips. The man who was too interesting, too marvelous to be true. "But why are you here? Why do you want this?" And behind these the silent question: *of all men you might have, why me?*

"Because it feels right," he replied, setting Norton's hand on his bare hip. "And because you asked me not to leave you."

"I did?"

"You did. So here I am. And here you are. And after what we went through, don't you think we deserve to be happy? Just for a little while."

"I am," Norton sighed as their bodies met, bare skin to bare skin. "You have no idea how happy you've made me."

Grinning wickedly, he tilted his hips, his ready cock sliding against Norton's own. "I have some idea." Norton moaned, his knees buckling. "Should I do that again?"

"Please, Emory, let's go to bed." *Before I fall to the floor and start begging. Before I catch fire where I stand.*

"Mmm, that's a fine thing to hear a man say. Say it again."

"Please, Emory. Take me to bed.

In answer he kissed him, another slow and lingering discovery of Norton's mouth, a sensual invasion surpassing every kiss before it. He wanted to feel that kiss everywhere, surrender to Emory's appetite, let himself be devoured. Surely that was Emory's plan, his kisses growing fiercer, his sparking hands caressing his neck, his back, his–

"Oh!" He tensed as Emory's fingers grazed the cleft of his buttocks, sending electric tingles through Norton's whole groin.

"Too much?" Emory asked.

"I don't know."

"What do you want, Norton?

"I–don't know. I'm sorry."

"How about if I tell you what I imagine?" Emory said, sliding his hands down Norton's flanks and up again. "I see you in my arms, our bodies close, just like this." He pulled Norton harder against him, their pricks rubbing against each other's belly. "And I kiss you and touch you until you beg me to let you release."

"Yes," Norton blurted, clutching Emory to him. "Please."

"Let's go to bed."

ELEVEN

Why had it seemed so complicated? What had ever made him hesitate? Now he could scarcely wait to get into bed, never mind that the counterpane lay on the floor and the pillows were crushed flat and the whole place smelled of bachelor. Emory Strike wanted him, wanted to touch him and kiss him. Norton had accepted long ago that any sentiments he felt for other men might never be returned. That he was not reward enough for all the dangers of living out such desires. To be wanted was strong drink and he was giddy with it.

And Emory's hands, by God... His every touch set off a storm of sensation, like the hot flare of his magic lived in his fingertips, building in dazzling waves until it became more than Norton could bear. He rolled away panting, his heart quivering in his chest.

"This is why I don't dare take a lover," Emory said with a rueful smile.

"Because they'd never let you leave the bedroom?"

He laughed softly. "Hardly. I've made fast enemies of a few men who thought I was aiming to kill them."

"Fools, all of them."

"I don't want to hurt you, Norton."

"You won't. You can't."

"I can," he answered, no humour in his tone. "I can stop a man's heart. End his life. I'm dangerous, Eckhart. It's wise to remember that."

"I don't care. I trust you." He brought Emory's hand to his lips and kissed it. Again, kissing his fingertips in turn, little sparks pricking his lips. Daring himself, he took the tip of Emory's forefinger in his mouth.

He groaned, his other arm tightening around Norton. "Damnation, Eckhart. You're going to break me," he breathed as Norton sucked his stiff finger deeper, a fizzing on his tongue and an answering sensation in his loins as their bodies rubbed together. Suddenly Emory cried out and pulled his hand from Norton's, not to evade him but to grasp his stiff and leaking cock.

Norton bit his lip, choking back his shout less it wake the world. Surely no ordinary touch could feel so luminous, so blazing hot yet pricking icily, sensation spreading from his loins in waves in time with Emory's heartbeat.

"Is it good?" he asked, and Norton nodded, though good was a wholly inadequate word for this infinity of feeling.

"I like how you look right now, 'Hart," Emory purred, tensing, releasing his grip. "I like how you move when I touch you." Norton groaned, his body moving without his volition, the twitch of his hips shoving his cock into Emory's firm grip. "That's it, Hart. That's what I want from you. I want to see your joy. I want to see your cream spurting over my hand."

"Yes! Please, I want–ahhh..." This, again and again, from this day forth. Not merely the hot thrill, the pleasure of release but that this man should be the one to bring him this pleasure, forever. A want so impossible that even at the height of passion, he felt his heart break.

"What was that you said about being quiet?"

"Hhnnn...sorry."

Laughing, Emory made to get off the bed. "Hang on, where are you going?" Norton asked. He tried to sit up but his slack muscles refused to cooperate.

"It's getting late."

"Please don't leave. Not yet." Not before he learned what it was like to be part of another man's pleasure, his joy. "Stay a little longer."

"Hart..."

"Anything you want, I want it too."

His lips trembling, Emory gazed at him, his expression unreadable in the softly flickering light. Then with a shuddering moan he fell on Norton, claiming his mouth in a kiss that transcended all before it. Ignoring the smear of sperm, Emory stretched his body over Norton's, the delirious weight of him crushing Norton into the mattress, stealing his breath, the iron shaft of Emory's cock hard against his belly.

Emory shifted downwards until the stiff length pressed between Norton's thighs. Though he'd claimed to want whatever Emory wanted, he couldn't control the instinctive closing of his legs.

"Damnation," Emory sighed, his eyes rolling closed.

"Is that good or bad?"

"Good. Really good."

"You mean you like this?" He pressed his thighs harder together and Emory groaned, nodded.

"Keep that up," he panted, his hips jerking, his cock slipping between Norton's thighs, slick with sperm and sweat. He was the most beautiful thing Norton had ever seen, lost in his pleasure, his mouth softly open, his eyes softly closed, his body flowing atop him, every place their skin touched illuminated by that tingling heat. Everything Emory wanted, he would give him, body and soul, their meeting an act of divine intervention, the reason for Norton's existence. As if the moment were ordained, Emory let out a moan, then sat back on his heels to grasp his cock and stroke himself to a shuddering climax, adding his hot semen to the mess on Norton's stomach, a holy act and pure debauch in one perfect moment.

Too perfect to last, as Emory dismounted, found his way across the room to the ewer on the table. Norton heard him hiss as he rinsed himself in the cold water. He came back with a scrap of towel for Norton, who dabbed ineffectively at his sticky torso while Emory hunted about for his clothes.

"Don't feel that you need to leave," he said, rolling towards Emory as he sat on the edge of the bed to pull on his tragically stained yellow trousers.

"You'll want to get some sleep."

"You don't need to leave for that to happen."

"As if we'd sleep," he said with a quiet laugh. "No, they'll need me soon, to strike the tents, pack the wagons."

"You're leaving tomorrow?"

"Most likely."

"When will you be back?"

"I don't know."

"Right," Norton said, a dreadful cold feeling growing in the pit of his stomach. He'd found a miracle and lost it, bared himself in the most intimate of ways to someone he had no hope of keeping. Emory was already at the door, his ruined jacket over his arm, a ruined look upon his face.

"I wish it didn't have to be this way," he said hoarsely. "I won't forget you."

"Emory..." But he was through the door and gone, and Norton was once more alone.

TWELVE

Predictably, despite it being close to four in the morning, Norton could not sleep. For sorrow, for shame, for fear that something terrible was happening to Emory at that very moment. A monster lurking under the bridge. That foul man Rotherhithe, bent on revenge, which was more likely and so even more frightening.

Day came and he was still awake, sick with worry and hating that he cared. Had Strike exploited him? He half wished it were so, for then he would be able to despise him, instead of wondering what he might have done to keep him here longer. Blunted, bumbling, he forced himself through his morning routine, though he eschewed Mrs. Selkie's zwieback and coffee so he needn't face her questioning.

He could do nothing to avoid his colleagues. Most had read the early papers, and those who hadn't had heard it from their fellows, and he had barely hung his hat before the first delegation was rapping at his door. He was partway through the tale when the next lot arrived and he was forced to start all over, and then again when the head of the department Mr. Bledsoe arrived with a pair of reporters from the Globe.

They took him to the specimen room, where one of the newspaper men dutifully sketched a crinoid fossil as if it was related to the monster, Norton's eyes drifting again and again to the window overlooking the field and the flags flying bravely above the big striped tent.

"I say, are you feeling alright, Mr. Eckhart?" asked the other reporter.

"Dr. Eckhart, if you please," he replied absently.

"Of course, Doctor, my mistake. I was asking you about this Mr. Strike you mentioned."

"Did you speak to him?"

"He was less forthcoming than you, sir. In fact I was wondering if you could clear up a few points for me."

"If he didn't tell you, why should I?"

"It's for the public good, sir."

"It's for their amusement. Batty Prof Battles 'Monster', that's what the morning edition said."

"Headlines are frequently sensationalized—"

"Do you believe me? Be honest."

"It's not a reporter's place to state their opinion, Doctor Eckhart."

"Then man to man. Do you believe me?" Why did he care? Because he was so close to disbelieving it himself. Where was the evidence? He was the same man he'd been yesterday. Other than muddy clothes and a lingering sensitivity, he had no proof that any of the ludicrous claims he'd made today were at all true.

"I believe that you saw something very strange last night, Doctor Eckhart," the reporter said with a smile, flipping to the next page in his little notebook. "As to what that strange thing is, your guess is as good as mine. Now, about Mr. Strike—"

Someone in the hall began to cough violently. No, it was Aurora, failing to be subtle as she pushed open the unlatched door. "Pardon me, gentlemen, but I need to speak with Dr. Eckhart immediately on an urgent matter."

"Can't it wait, Miss Bramble?" Bledsoe asked tersely, for he and Aurora agreed on precisely nothing.

"I'm dreadfully sorry, Doctor," she said, dropping a tiny curtsey and ignoring the newspaper men, who had both sat up straighter on hearing her illustrious last name. "But it can't be helped. Come along, Doctor, I'll explain on the way."

"What's the matter?" he asked in a whisper as they hurried along the corridor.

"Nothing's the matter. I just thought you needed rescuing."

"You're such a blessing."

"Eck, what happened to you last night?" she asked as he stepped ahead to open the door to the stairwell for her.

"You haven't heard?"

"Yes, but that's not all that happened. Or you'd be much more excited."

"Would I?"

"Yes, all right, you were in some danger," she said blithely as they started down the stairs, "but I'd like to think that were it I to face a fearsome creature from the dawn of time I might at least be a little curious. Instead you look like you've had your heart broke—" She stopped, one foot in the air, and grabbed his sleeve. "Oh Eck, you didn't. How did you manage that?"

He wanted to deny it but there was no one he trusted more. "I don't know. I...I don't know what I expected."

"Was it someone from that circus?" He nodded miserably. She sighed, pity pulling down the corners of her mouth. "Eckhart, did you fall in love with the lion tamer?"

"They don't have a lion. And I'm not in love."

"You wish you weren't."

"If you're being pedantic."

"I'm being honest." They fell silent as another pair of feet sounded on the stairs, giving Norton time to reflect on Aurora's joking question. Not the trapeze girl or an orange seller but the lion tamer. Was he really that transparent?

He followed her meekly to her miniscule office, which he suspected had once been a supply closet. It required some bold maneuvering of Aurora's underskirts for her to fit behind the desk. "Are you going to tell me about him or do I have to draw it out like a bad tooth?" she said once he was settled in the facing chair, his knees pressed against the front of her desk.

Again he thought of denying everything, but she'd have it out of him in the end. "I don't know why he gave me a second thought," he said, his heartbeat slowing as her expression showed none the derision and disgust he had feared. "He was a showman, you see? I told him to his face I thought he was a faker. He didn't even want for my help. But if I hadn't followed when he was after those thieves, he might be dead now. And I let him...but then he left me and...By God, you must think I'm pathetic."

"Not a bit," she said gently as he searched his pockets for his handkerchief, sniffing back the betraying tears. "Not pathetic. Exhausted, and badly frightened, and full of regret."

"I don't regret it, though. I'd do it again."

"You surely regret some part of it, even if only that it ended as it did." She offered her own handkerchief and he dabbed at his face. "Have you eaten anything today?"

"No," he said, feeling like a child, wishing he still was one, so that someone else might be responsible.

"Let's go to the commissary and get you a bun and cup of chocolate, shall we?"

He preceded her into the corridor to allow her to get around the desk without worrying about discretion. A miscalculation for there was Captain Pendleton, exiting Monkman's office.

"Eckhart!" he hollered, waving his cane to catch his eye like they stood on a crowded train platform and not an empty hall. "What's this I hear about you fighting sea serpents?"

"The papers have somewhat sensationalized my involvement," Norton said as the Captain came stumping towards him, the shoe on his false leg whapping against the floorboards.

"Never mind the papers. Come to dinner next week and you may tell us in your own words. You as well, Miss Bramble," he said as Aurora joined them. "I would be honored if you would grace our table with your scintillating intellect."

"With my what?"

"She'd be happy to," Norton blurted.

"No, I wouldn't—want to offend your other guests, that is," she finished, flashing Norton a dark look.

"You never mind them, Miss Bramble," the Captain said in a conspiratorial tone. "Though in the name of keeping the peace it would do for you to have a chaperone."

"I'll squire her," Norton offered.

"Excuse me, squire?" she said to him through clenched teeth.

"Excellent," said the Captain, grinning broadly. "See you Thursday."

"You owe me," she muttered to Norton as the man clomped away.

"I do." He owed her more than she would ever know.

THIRTEEN

He endured a week of celebrity, but there was only so much to be said and only so many people to hear it, and by month's end it had become a mildly amusing inside joke around the department. He avoided the specimen room, for he too often found himself gazing hopelessly out the window. Other faculty were planning summer camps, Monkman bound for the rich hunting grounds of the eastern Rockies, where new specimens, new species seemed to fall from the crumbling hillsides into the discoverers' hands.

"Come with me," Monkman said to him one afternoon in the library as they surveyed the pages of a new folio from a dig in the Dakota Territory.

"Where?"

"To the North-West. It's a new El Dorado," he said with a spark in his bright blue eyes. Norton used to find that spark so enticing. Now and then had pictured Monkman at camp, dressed down to his undershirt, sweat beading his forehead as he laid into the rock face with a pick-axe.

"Perhaps," he replied. "I have nearly exhausted our collection of crinoids."

"Never mind those sea-weeds of yours," Monkman said, prodding him with his elbow. "This is a chance to make your mark. Discover yourself an Eckmanisaurus."

"Imagine that."

"Do let me know," Monkman said, bending over the map again. "I'll be leaving within the week."

"So soon?"

"It will take some time to get there. And the winters are said to top any of ours."

Norton left him and made his way downstairs. He had made a habit of checking his mailbox twice a day, unwilling to admit to anyone but himself that he was hoping for a letter from Emory. *Dr. Eckhart, Trinity College, Toronto*: no postal office on the continent could mistake such an address. A postcard, a telegraph...any sign that he'd been anything more than a passing amusement.

Aurora was in the foyer, concluding one of her tours of the college, a duty she accepted as payment for her unwarranted attendance. He sidled around the group of matriculating preparatory school students and their parents, whose expressions ranged from bold enthusiasm to yawning boredom. Flicking through his copy of the Royal Society's latest journal, he lingered in the mail room until they dispersed.

"Has Monkman been onto you?" Aurora asked once she'd joined him.

"Is everyone against me now?"

"I'm not against you, I'm for you," she said, flipping through her letters, addressed to her masculine pseudonym Armistead Burton. "It will give you something to look forward to."

"You may be right."

"Have you a better idea for keeping yourself occupied over the summer break?"

"You know I don't."

She glanced towards the door, but the foyer was empty. "I know you wonder who is on your side," she said quietly. "But trust me when I say that I am. And it's hurt me so to watch you pine."

"I'm not pining."

"Yes, and neither were Tristan and Iseult," she said dryly. "Eck, I want for you to be happy. No matter who it is that makes you so."

He doesn't make me happy. I met him just the once. We haven't spoken since. "Why do I still care?" he found himself asking.

"There must have been some feeling between you," she said, gripping his arm. "Don't mistake his absence for a lack of caring. We're all victims of circumstance, dear Norton. If you weren't beholden to the college, would you have gone with him?"

"Yes."

"Then don't presume he doesn't feel the same. Keep an open mind, Eck. You may surprise yourself."

Perhaps she was right. Perhaps it was mere circumstance that had come between them. Was there a way he might reach out to Emory? Enquire at post offices, put up a notice, make his needs known without compromising their safety. Admit publicly that he wanted another chance to know him.

"Come along, Eck," she said, plucking at his sleeve. "Take me to lunch. Spare me Professor Wooten's company, he's convinced I shall perish of dining alone."

He offered his arm and they left the mailroom. The foyer was happily empty of prospective students though their shoe prints lingered on the marble floor. Near the door, a man in a faun linen dittoe suit was perusing the list of faculty names on the board by the entrance. He straightened, revealing a bi-coloured face that split into a joyful smile. "Eckhart! What luck."

"How…why…you…" A great wave of emotion, of hope and despair and loneliness, rose from the depths of Norton's soul as Emory Strike came towards him, glowing with joy. Really glowing, a haze of heat and light haloing his hands and face.

"It's him," Aurora hummed, going up on tiptoe to reach Norton's ear. "Don't tell me it isn't."

"It is. It's him."

"Then get ready to introduce me, dear biscuit-head."

He jerked away to stare at her. "What do you mean, introduce?"

"Am I not your friend and confidante?" she said, batting her lashes at him like he was any other man.

"Yes, but…" Too late, for here was Strike, standing before him, and it took all of Norton's strength not to throw his arms around him and kiss away the weeks of wanting, say with touch what he did not know how to say in words. Emory was as handsome as ever, and perhaps he felt the same, his smile luminous, his jaw trembling.

"Miss Aurora Bramble," Norton blurted, his voice cracking for she had pinched him quite hard under the arm. "May I present Mr. Emory Strike. Master of the Marvelous."

"How do you do, Mr. Strike," she said, extending her hand.

"Quite well, Miss Bramble," he replied with a little bow as he gripped her hand confidently.

"Now that we've done with the formalities," she said, "you must call me Aurora, and know that I am Eck's very best friend. So be kind to him or I'll make your life exceedingly difficult."

"I shall, Miss Bramble," he said, winking at Norton. "Beg your pardon, Aurora."

"Why are you here?" Norton asked him.

"I came to see you."

"You didn't."

"Oh?" Laughter in his eyes, Emory set his hands on his hips. "Then tell me, why am I here?"

"I don't know."

Aurora coughed conspicuously. "Might I suggest you gentlemen continue this fascinating conversation behind closed doors?"

FOURTEEN

They went up by the back stairs to lessen the chance of having to speak to anyone. "Whatever happened to that thing of Ignatio's?" Norton asked Emory as they climbed.

"I don't know yet."

"Yet?"

"That's what I've been doing, hunting for it," he said, speaking half over his shoulder to Aurora behind them. "The circus folded after word got round, and O'Malley offered."

"O'Malley?" asked Norton.

"Erin O'Malley, also known as Professor Ignatio."

"But Mr. Strike, isn't that creature terribly dangerous?" Aurora said, possibly for Norton's benefit as she'd never concerned herself with such in the past.

"It might be if I'd got within twenty miles of the thing. It's always gone by the time I get there."

"Thank the Lord," Norton said under his breath.

"I'm not spoiling for the fight, that's for certain."

Aurora's little hutch was the first door they passed and she bid them good day and shut herself inside. And then it was only Emory, and Norton had to get him inside a room with a door as soon as possible so he could kiss him.

"Which office is yours?" Emory asked as they started down the corridor keeping a discrete gap between them.

"There's not much to see in there."

"It's as good a place to start the tour as anywhere."

"As you like."

They reached his room without meeting anyone else. Redding had been offered tenure at the end of the term and had moved to a better office, and Norton had enjoyed the last few days of solitude. Unlike his home, he kept his office tidy, as so many of the papers belonged to other people who expected them back in one piece. He closed the door, then turned the lock, for too many of his colleagues treated his cheerfulness as an open invitation.

He stood with his hand on the latch, fighting a sudden illogical fear that he had imagined the last ten minutes and he would turn to find the office empty. It wasn't possible that Strike was here, that he'd come back just to see him. But there was the scent of him, of petrichor and hot sweat, and Norton turned to ask for that kiss he wanted, and...

Here it was, that kiss, as Emory pulled him into his arms and brought their lips together. Such magic in Emory's touch, its searing, tingling, sweetness, the hunger of his kiss. A kiss that went on and on, until the world faded from significance and all that was left was this man and this kiss.

"You really are here to see me," Norton murmured as Emory began to nuzzle at his neck.

"I am."

"I haven't stopped thinking about you. I worried..."

He raised his head. "Worried?"

"That something had happened to you. That I'd never see you again."

"Dear Hart…"

"That. To never hear you say my name like that again. You can't know what this means to me, to find you here. I've felt like half a man since we said goodbye. Not because I wanted someone to depend on, but because I regret that I have so much feeling for you but wasn't brave enough to express it."

"You hardly know me," Emory murmured, his words at odds with his actions as his arms tightened around Norton.

"Maybe so, but I know this to be true. You said yourself there's more to this world than what we see with our eyes. Being with you feels more right than anything I've ever done. The biggest risk I could ever take but absolutely worth it."

"Damnation, Hart…"

"I don't know how we'll manage but I want you to know that I'm yours, whenever you want me."

"I do."

They kissed again and more fiercely, clawing at each other's clothes, shameless in their disregard for the world on the other side of one thin door. He did not care, not about his reputation, or his safety, or anything beyond this man's embrace.

Something hard struck the back of his legs: his desk, blessedly clear of paper, and he lay back, bringing Emory with him. For once he was going to something uncalculated, not merely break from convention but break laws and moral standards, make himself and his lover happy, without remorse.

More brave thoughts which fled from his mind at a sturdy knock on the door. Emory flung himself around the desk and disappeared under it. "Can I help you?" Norton said loudly, tucking in his shirt as he went to the door.

"I wanted a word," Monkman said. "And who were you talking to?"

"Myself." He looked about but the room appeared empty, so he opened the door, keeping his foot wedged behind it. "I do that now and then. You should know that before we end up stuck on some mountainside together and you think I've lost my mind."

"Right." Monkman said, his brow furrowed. "What's wrong with your collar?"

Norton felt his throat, straightening his shirt collar to cover the wet place where Emory had been nibbling. "My, I am a mess, aren't I?"

"Are you ill?"

"Never better."

"Look, about that camp—"

"I'll let you know tomorrow."

"Do that," Monkman said. "I'd like to organize supplies and such as soon as I can."

"Of course. See you then." He shut the door, waiting for Monkman's footsteps to die away before locking it, for fear of being too blatant. He returned to his chair and fell into it with a sigh.

Crouching beneath the skirted desk, Emory laughed quietly. "Did I even need to hide?"

"Oh you did, he'd have been here for hours."

"What was he talking about?" he asked, shuffling forward to rest his elbows on Norton's knees.

"A research trip. Out west."

"Then it's good I got here when I did." He laid his hands flat on Norton's thighs. A spangling heat began to spread, up his legs and deep inside him as Emory slid his hands towards Norton's crotch.

His rising prick pressing against the front of his trousers, he slid down in his seat. "Yes," he murmured as Emory palmed him through the clinging linen. "Very good."

"Is that door locked?" Emory said, running his thumb lightly over Norton's cods. He nodded, his tongue dry, thoughts aswirl, logic and restraint like dust on the wind as Emory slipped the fingers of his other hand between the buttons of Norton's fly.

"Is this too much?" he murmured as Norton hissed in a breath, grabbing the arms of his chair.

"Yes, but don't stop."

"Hart, I've thought about you so often," he said, tugging open his buttons. "All the ways I want to know you, how I wished I'd had more time with you."

"You have me now." Now and forever, his heart, his every cell aflame with wild desire as Emory spread his trousers open and bared his aching cock.

"Damnation..." Emory breathed, sitting back.

"What's wrong?"

"Me for thinking I didn't want this. For thinking it wasn't going to kill me to give you up."

He had no reply, needed none, as Emory gripped his leaking cock then leaned in to taste the fluid pearling from the tip. And then it was all he could do not to shout aloud, both hands clamped over his gaping mouth as Emory's quicksilver tongue played up and down his length, every stroke a shooting star, the hot clasp of Emory's hand an inferno of pressure and pleasure. Every day and lonesome night that had passed since they met was a small price to pay for this wealth, this sublime gift, this joy.

He looked down as Emory looked up. Their eyes met, and Emory chose that moment to take Norton in his mouth. Pleasure flared through him, burning away his last restraint, and he bit his hand to keep from sobbing aloud as Emory sucked him deeper. Deeper still, until his lips met his encircling fingers, wetting them so they slid along Norton's shaft. More, Norton rocking to meet his lover's mouth. His lover, his love, his Emory, returned to him, and the joy and the sweet sensations became one and the same as he climaxed.

He should have given warning, he realized too late, as Emory fell back, coughing and wiping his mouth. But when he slid forward in the chair Emory rose on his knees to kiss him, his lips salted by Norton's spend.

Clearing his throat, Emory got to his feet. "That's the second pair of trousers you've seen me ruin, " he said with a laugh, brushing ineffectually at the dust on his knees.

"I'll start carrying a cushion with me."

He laughed again as Norton stood up to button his fly. Midday assignations were all very well but he didn't relish trying to make it out of the building all red faced and sticky handed without being seen by any number of overly curious people.

"You realize I can't go with Monkman now," he said as he tried to rebend the wire of his neck-stock.

"What if I came with?" Emory said, perched on the front of Redding's now empty desk.

"Why would you do that?"

"Other than the obvious? Because I'm tired of O'Malley and his money. I never wanted anything to do with that damned egg of his. If I'm going to stump around the backwoods, getting bit by flies and insulted by idiots...I might do so in better company."

"There will be several idiots on Monkman's crew, if he stays true to form."

"Of course, if you'd rather, or we could stay in town and do our own exploration."

"Oh? Oh. We could."

"Perform some rigorous science," Emory said, reaching for his hand to pull him near.

"We'll need to conduct numerous trials," Norton said, settling between Emory's spread thighs.

"Lay out some hard facts."

"Seek an inarguable conclusion."

"A what?"

"A good ending."

"Yes. A very good ending."

Those thighs were now wrapped around Norton's hips, and so naturally they kissed. A miraculous act of the everyday, a gift of the divine, a sign of love. Hidden in plain sight, but he only had to look at this man in his arms to see a miracle.

JOIN THE READERS CLUB FOR MORE *TALES OF ELSE-WHEN*

ALSO BY

THE OLD RAZZLE DAZZLE: a London Hustle book

Two romances, two eras & too much drama when an aging theatre director becomes the unlikely mentor to a talented young singer in this Edwardian-era novel of loss and redemption.
"An R-rated queer historical Hallmark romance" (Britt Hanowell, Boundless Words)

AN INCONVENIENT EARL: a Gay Regency Romance

Is his lordship's dearest wish about to come true? Or is the only man he trusts now his enemy?
A passionate tale of freedom, forgiveness, and saying exactly the wrong thing in bed.

ABOUT THE AUTHOR

Author, blogger, and general nuisance Will Forrest writes unusual (and usually queer) Historical and Paranormal Romances with a dash of mischief and mayhem.

Will grew up on a steady diet of Douglas Adams and classic 90s bodice rippers, and has a diploma of fashion design, a degree in social theory, and a bad habit of changing careers, life goals, and continents. Currently Will lives in a very warm part of Canada with three lovely humans and a succession of martyred houseplants.

www.willforrest.com